Whit

a not entirely fictional mystery

by

SIMON COLE

Some other books by the same author:

Stillness in Mind - a companion to mindfulness, meditation, living
(Changemakers Books, 2014)

Pathways - humanity's search for its soul
(Amazon, 2017, 2019)

Just Be Here - the guide to musicking mindfulness
(Amazon, 2020)

Copyright © 2022 Simon Cole

All rights reserved. This book or any portion thereof may not be reproduced or used in any manner whatsoever without the express permission of the publisher except for the use of brief quotations in a book review or scholarly Author's journal *for Barbara in memory*

In 1948 the French composer Olivier Messiaen completed his Turangalîla Symphony. It is a work of 10 movements lasting around 80 minutes. It is sometimes said that the name he gave to it might be understood as an allegory for 'love song'. Messiaen himself said that he combined two Sanskrit words, *turanga* meaning the flow of time, constant movement and rhythm, and *lîla* which means the continuing dance of creation, the play of life and death.

an epilogue and a prologue

She was 104 when she died.

I wasn't there.

No-one was.

Not because she was a neglected old lady that no-one cared about. Simply, they weren't there at the time.

And even if they had been physically present, though they weren't, they still would not have been there *in* the time, the time when that life actually ended, if it did, with all its traces which might have been but weren't and all its courses which were but easily might not have been and all its cast of characters, a lot of whom I knew or knew of, and others which appeared from the shadows and I wondered whether they were really there or somewhere else or not at all, and all the scenes and props and roles, and the confusion of sets and settings when the action moved, sometimes you could see it but sometimes it was offstage and reported, and then you have to trust the word passed down across the terraces of history, the hardships, the joys, the resentments, the hopes, the terror, the humanity, the resilience - a passage of 104 years through who can say how many acts and worlds, and somewhere back along the way, still tolling, the bourdon bell which marked the tide of war.

Perhaps it seems a little strange to start with her death, but that is where the view is from. Everything that was going to happen has completed. No more now. It's all over and it's all there. Which doesn't mean we can know it for what it was, because time is like distance and obscures detail. It also obscures meaning and connections and thereby can even re-draw the landscape. But unlike the mountain-side which displays a single aspect from a distance, but with our footfall on its contours reveals a much more complex set of features, another life's landscape is as we see it, in 2D, the 3D no more than conjecture, and the whole only as we *think* we see it.

It is certain that no physical acquaintance is possible, for in death it occupies untouchable space. Separate from us. No, we can only look, and wonder - what might have been no longer relevant to a search for what was.

Surely, now, the connection is lost.

Surely, now, it is what it was, and cannot be again.

~~~

"All the world's a stage" the Bard said, "and all the men and women merely players." Sometimes, though, I wondered whether this analogy went far enough. Yes, there was the stage and the players, but then there was the play itself and somehow that was written. So, is there another presence? Who wrote Barbara's play? And then that inside/outside existential question - is the world the play, or is the play the world? Are we not each one of us the stage for others' plays and they for ours?

A rich and varied cast of characters walked on her stage. I only knew a handful, but they were all there somewhere in one of those rooms and had their space. Did I have a space too? I seemed to be in the play somewhere, though never noticed, it appeared, never part of any action, wandering among the scenes, an invisible visitor in worlds I could never know. And each world a land that I would never see. They floated past like islands that you just glimpse through the mist, Norway, India, Austria, South Africa. I cannot know which of all these countries she set foot in - if any, for I never found a passport - but one place kept appearing through the mist.

Vienna - aloof, grandiose Vienna. Watching. Home of international peace-brokering, deal-making, the Prater, spies, the Ring Strasse, pure white porcelain...

Yes, that white porcelain.

I remember on an early visit to the city going into a slightly up-market collectibles shop just off the Ring and being stunned by the variety of exquisite porcelain on display, most of it delicately though, to my taste, rather garishly painted, but then as I went further into the shop - was this the inner sanctum? - across one wall, not crowded together like the pieces elsewhere, but spaced elegantly, each standing on its own glass plinth somehow magically projecting from a wall of midnight blue, an array of dazzling pure white shining figurines, mostly animals, domestic and wild, around six inches tall, some slightly larger. The effect was like so many stars glinting from distant galaxies. There was one plinth empty and an assistant who was following me and noticed that I had paused with some interest, bustled around behind a counter and quickly found its occupant, a cat, I think, but I paid no great attention.

Many years later, in one of the rooms, I found a small veneered box of the sort we used to call a 'deed box' with its recessed hinged lid locked (but fortunately the miniature key still in place), and in it was a business card from KÄRNTNER ANTIQUITARIAT, WIEN. I thought it might have been the same collectibles shop, but I wasn't sure. There were also two old photographs in the box: one a very faded black and white photograph of a nineteenth century steamship, two tall funnels and schooner-rig, probably a souvenir postcard for passengers, with the caption *Union-Castle Liner, "Saxon"*, and the other with no inscription at all - this latter was a studio photograph from the nineteenth century of a young man of around 19 years with confident expression and symmetrical swept-back hair, formal high-collar shirt and tie and flamboyant baggy jacket, his pose insouciant but purposive with his forearm resting on a high-backed chair.

There were also two envelopes in the box. One was addressed in what I thought was a woman's hand: "Barbara, Cleeve Hill Park, Frenchay, Bristol, England". The printed heading at the top read:

Evangelischer Verein für Innere Mission: Mädchenheim
Evangelisches Krankenhaus, Wien-Alsergrund

an epilogue and a prologue

The envelope had not been opened and I decided to leave it that way, at least for now, but I could read a part of the postmark, which said VIII.1953. The other was slightly larger than an ordinary letter and addressed to 'Mr Francis Cole' (my grandfather) and with the postmark date still clearly visible: 30th August 1902. I recognised the handwriting as that of my Grandaunt Louie, my grandfather's youngest sister. Inside the envelope was another studio photograph, this one of a young African woman wearing a striking white and black dress. It was an old photograph and below the image was the photographer's inscription: Jakins Willard & Co (Oxford Street, East London).

There seemed to be nothing to link any of the items, but separately in a cupboard, inside a marquetry box which contained mainly sewing implements and threads, I found another faded black and white photograph of an African woman, sitting, holding a baby. Comparing this with the photograph in the envelope, I was fairly certain they were the same person.

~~~

Author's journal 6th December 2021:

What gives us the sense that our lives have a course, not pre-destination or anything like that, but a feeling of cohesiveness? OK, same body, but psychological not physical this sense, maybe even spiritual, like some pattern of how we work... and that this is recognisable as 'us'? In some respects it doesn't seem to fit the evidence, since most of what happens to us is connected with other people and often after something has happened, we know that in a similar situation some other time we will be different <u>because</u> of what happened before... because of them, the other people, almost like a bit of them is now a bit of us.

And if sometimes, why not all the time?

the first room

<u>Letter from Barbara to Peter 3rd May 1948</u>

Dear Peter,

I assume you got my last letter. I have waited 8 weeks for a reply and none has come, so I decided to write again in the hope that you will realise that I write for a reason. I know we must seem a long way away to you, far enough for it to not really matter what happens here, but we are still family and I need someone to talk to. You can never talk to Mother, as you know, well, no, you can talk to her can't you, but I can't, I'm a woman and a daughter. Worst of all worlds. What about Norman, you'll say? And you are right, but you are wrong. So, are you going to exert yourself and pick up a pen and do something useful in one of your long leisurely evenings? After all, there's not much else to do, surely? Don't you have servants to look after everything out there?

I'll come straight to the point. I'm lost. If, again, you are thinking, what about Norman?

Well he is part of the being lost. Unfortunately. I really mean unfortunately, because nothing is his fault. It's all mine. Why did I think it would work getting married during the war? I was fully occupied, work during the day and then every night out (did I tell you I drove ambulances?), and Norman doing his stuff evenings as well, he was in the ARP[1], so we couldn't have a real life. Why do it? Comfort, companionship, someone to come home to (if you were lucky enough to come home), to know there was something that was yours in the world, that couldn't be touched. All of those. But why actually get married? Well we both know the answer to that. Mother. I don't know why I thought it could be a normal married life, home of our own, two kids, all that. Nothing was normal back then. I got home from the office around half past five, changed, had some tea, listened to the news, put his tea out ready if he was going to be late, and then I had to leave again by 7 because my duty started at 8, but you had to allow extra time to get anywhere once the blitz started. The duty ended at midnight, if I was lucky. You could be out somewhere and not be able to get back, or

---

[1] Acronym for Air Raid Precautions, who were volunteer wardens.

the first room

if it was a really bad one and someone couldn't get in or there was a late call, it could be 2 or later before you left to go home.

Are you thinking, but that's all over now the war's over? It ought to be, I know. And it is, so long as you ignore the derelict bomb sites and the house next door which isn't there and the rationing and the identity cards and the cold. But thinking about it now, we never started married life, Norman and I, and what was us has gone and now there <u>is</u> nowhere to start. (I said we never started, I mean we started as man and wife and I expected to have a child by now, but nothing.) Now there is nowhere to start and even to think of starting seems almost inappropriate. I listen to the news and read the papers and mostly that's all crowing about glorious victory and the lads coming home, or it's how Britain is building for a glorious future and taking care of the people, or else it's inane political arguing about the mines or the national health, when they should be pulling together, and you almost don't notice the pieces about how bad it is on the Continent. Millions of refugees just wandering, people dying of starvation, whole cities just rubble, the occupation, our occupying forces, corruption, the communists, spies from all sides, cells of Nazi hardliners still sabotaging, killing our boys and sometimes ours have to shoot ordinary people! The BBC and the papers don't tell you about that side of things, but I can't put it out of my head, because I know.

Oh dear, I wasn't meaning to go down that road. Now I am worried that you are going to think I am a fraud. Why couldn't I tell you straight out? Not about Norman at all, not even about our unreal beginning in the war. I could have been honest at the start. No, I don't believe you will think bad of me. I don't think you will, not you. Perhaps it's different for you. Is it different for you? (I don't expect you to answer that, no reason why you should, but I have always wondered. I have no idea what that's like.)

Alright, here it is. His name is Hugh. He is an officer, something to do with the Field Security Section, whatever that is, and he is in Vienna with the British Army Occupation Force. (I probably shouldn't say that. I hope no-one sees your letters.) We met by accident. Norman was working and I had gone to Bath just for something different. Get away from the mess here. Bath was never bombed, you know, or not like Bristol. I cycled, would you believe? When I got there, I just wandered around and went into the Pump Rooms for tea. I suppose I didn't know anywhere else and Mother and I had been in there a few times (you know what she's like about Bath being so elegant), anyway there wasn't much choice. It wasn't like the old days, but they had managed to open up in one half of the ballroom. All the tables were taken and I was on my way out again when this young military chap raised his hand and motioned me to the other side of his table. And I just sat down! Can you believe? Me? I think the war has made us different. Our characters. We seem to just do things without thinking now.

He was going back to Vienna that night, I suppose that's why he was in uniform, so after tea we strolled around for a couple of hours and then had another tea in a little place in Northumberland Square. He told me things about Vienna, how it had been a wonderful city before the war, but now so much destruction and not enough food (the Russians have all the best farmlands), everywhere people starving and cold, and the central part of the city run by a joint council of the four armies, full of agents and intrigue and disappearances, as if there is a new war now between the four that won the last one. That's why his lot are in there.

Eventually I realised how late it was and how was I going to get home? No chance to get back before Norman got in from work. I panicked. No need, Hugh's train was leaving from Bristol and he had a borrowed car, so he took me back with my bicycle strapped on the boot, but I still had the problem of explaining to Norman. It just wasn't me to be so disorganised as not to be home for him. But you are only in Hugh's line of duty if you are resourceful. We were nearly home. He stopped, took the bike off the back, got out his knife and put a gash in the front tyre so that it immediately deflated. "That's why you're late", he said and we parted. I scurried up the hill. I think he waited at the bottom until I disappeared. We didn't even hug! (Not that I hug, as you know, but the war might have changed that too, who knows?) Before, I would have been horrified if someone deliberately damaged something like that and walked away pleased with themselves. But now? Inside I was smiling and I was impressed because he was someone who didn't worry.

I'll have to finish this later. I'm trembling.

...

That was 3 weeks ago. I have been on tenterhooks waiting for a letter to come - like a little girl waiting for Father Christmas. It was going to be tricky, but I told him to use a Post Office, not our local one, the one down on the Gloucester Road. And then I feel silly, going in to ask. I didn't really think he would write, but I set it up with them all the same, because what would I do if he wrote straightaway? Anyway, nothing has appeared. I think I'm relieved. That's what I tell myself anyway.

I need help, Peter! I didn't think I would ever ask for that, but I feel as if I have landed in a foreign country without a map or a compass and all the signposts have gone and the people too. Is it the war or is it love? If it's love, then I never felt it before and now I feel very guilty because Norman is a brick and tries so hard for me. I can't let this go on. Can I? Dare I? It isn't right, I know. But I'm not sure whether that's not one of the signposts that's missing too - what's right and what's not.

Oh dear, oh dear. I am going to stop. I hope there is something you can say. There usually is. In your ebullient way. But that's alright. I don't mind that, it's you. Why do women instinctively feel safe with, well, you know? You don't have to answer that, it was a silly question.

I am exhausted and I haven't even asked about you, but I hope you will tell me anyway.

Your loving sister,

Barbara

Letter from Peter to Barbara 29th May 1948

Dear Barbara,

'Queer' is the word, Sis, and you don't have to be so coy, just don't go blurting it out everywhere because I don't want to end up in Reading gaol, or any other gaol come to that. Certainly not an Indian gaol. Anyway nothing happens, I don't have anyone, just a friend I write to.

Now that's out the way, let's talk about you.

My first reaction is have a great time when you can, free fun is always the best fun, that is if your Hugh ever makes it back to England again. Because Vienna is dangerous and it's not just Austrians and renegades who are getting killed. I had a letter a bit ago from an old comrade who was re-posted to his home unit in England and then sent to Austria.

So look after your heart, dear sister, because there might not be anyone else around to do it. That said, hasn't the war, especially what <u>you</u> did in it, changed your outlook? To take what's given when it comes because tomorrow, or even in a few minutes, it might not be there and neither might you. OK, if you're dead you don't know you've missed out, but you can't cash in your chips in your coffin.

You know I'm not the person to come to for wise advice. I live with whatever comes up. I always have. Anytime I've had anything, I've ended up losing it. And <u>my</u> day of *reckoning is still to come: Your "foreign country without signposts and people" is coming for me as well, just not quite yet. They still need us at the moment, but I give it 3 years, 4 at the most.*

I'm not as unsympathetic as I sound. You had the worst deal after our father died. You were his favourite that's for certain, he took you out on your own and bought you things. That's not something he ever knew himself, being the favourite I mean - as far as his father was concerned he had killed the favourite! (You know, the uncle Harry no-one talked about, who died somehow in South Africa during the Boer War.) Then, poor man, Father that is, in the space of a month he was gone. I do wonder what that was like for you, to see him go down so quickly. Different for me six years younger, for me the worst part was hardly being allowed to see him, but when you're that age you just accept that some things happen behind closed doors and you're not allowed to be a part. And then afterwards you see the world's different and that's how it is now, so you just get on with it. But you,

you couldn't just get on with it. From the day he died it must have seemed you lost your life as well. Thinking about it now, it's as if the Aunts sacrificed you. Mother closed down, so they had to do something. We were easy, because they could do something practical like get us away to school, but someone had to look after Mother and it wouldn't be them.

What was it like when we were all away at school? Did she really walk you up to the cemetery every day? That was miles. And just you and her in the house until we got back for the holidays. I'm very sorry Ba. You paid for us. And you paid later as well, working and handing over your wages. I suppose, if nothing else, the war when it came let you grow up, if grow up means grow away. But why get married in the middle of it all?

Why am I going through all this? Probably because it's the only thing I can think of doing. No, not just that. It's the first time it has felt I could do it. I never really thought about anyone else, hardly noticed anyone else because the three of you looked after everything I needed, and I got the best deal of the four of us and I never had to work. Then in the army (officer by a fluke because of College), and posted to India. A 'good war', they say, don't they? And so long as you knew when to look the other way it was. (I thank my lucky stars I never got sent to Burma.)

Now look at me. Mind, I thought that was a bit unfair, your bit about having servants to do everything. But, yes, it's true. And I don't have to physically do anything. I go around all day making sure everybody else does what they are supposed to, checking we get enough pickers if there's illness around, making sure the dryers get repaired promptly when they go wrong, making sure the shipments go out. But they know their jobs and they have to earn money. I wonder sometimes whether sooner or later we'll start to get sabotage and unrest. They don't like us here and they don't want us now after independence, but for the moment they have no choice. Our days are numbered though.

Here I go, I'm off on my own stuff as usual. I was really meaning to say I can see why you've ended up swaying one way and the other, and I don't think you should feel bad or guilty or anything else. Though I do reckon you need to stop and reflect. Buy yourself some time. Nothing <u>has</u> to happen immediately, so nothing should. If you write to this Hugh, keep it formal at least until you've met him again, which I can't imagine will be soon. Find the old Ba, who knew the "proper" way to behave and expected everybody else to keep to her standards. There was no taking liberties with her!

I'm going to finish. I've got someone coming round for the evening, so I'll send the boy down to the office with this and you'll get it as quickly as can be.

Go easy and write again when you can manage. Life goes on.

All the best,
Peter

~~~

The rooms were not actual rooms, at least not all of them, they were more like the backdrop and props left on the stage after a scene has finished. Some of them might be used again in another scene, or the same setting might be used later, or the stage revolves and the whole atmosphere is transformed in a few short moments.

For the bird of passage that I seemed to be, the fascination was in the knowing that all these sets were for one stage and all the scenes one play. Even when a play's run is over, the stage still remains, bare now, but with the imprint of all those feet; and in the end the scenery, the props, even the costumes get re-used. Nothing dies completely. And if nothing dies completely, everything connects, somewhere.

the second room

He had been sitting in the entrance hall of the Beach Hotel for most of 4 days now. Occasionally he went out, presumably to get some food at one of the stores in the town, and then came back and sat again. Sometimes when he came back there weren't any seats so he found a coffee table to use, but the management usually objected, moving him outside, and then he sat on the steps of the hotel's bar on the corner. Only a few people knew, mostly by hearsay, why he was there all the time, but it didn't make much difference to the way they gave him a wide berth, just like everyone did. It was clear to almost everyone that he wasn't a holiday-maker or a tripper like they all were - his clothes gave that away, not so much because of the complete lack of any appropriate formality, though that too of course, but because they were worn and dusty and looked as if they came from somewhere not part of their world, at least not any longer. The occasional person who heard him say the odd word could have noticed his English accent, which might have turned their mind to thoughts of the Empire dealing with the rebellion, but now it was well into 1902 and it was time to move on. (This despite the nightmare having only just ended, for the final agreement had been signed no more than a few days before.) Colonial society down here on the coast had not been that much affected - occasionally a bit close for comfort perhaps, but so quickly it seems the shutters of normality close out yesterday's troubles.

As it was, most people presumed he had come from a war front somewhere. (A few khakis had been staying in East London over the last couple of years - the resort offered a brief respite from the stress of ambush and skirmish and it was not so long ago that whole units with equipment were disembarking here and moving on north and east. Besides that, only a few months ago the Boers were rampant not far away in the Eastern Cape itself, so it all fitted.) One or two of the hotel residents might even have paused to wonder if there hadn't been two of them together sometimes, but few gave that a second thought.

When he wasn't sitting at the Beach Hotel overcome by feelings of remorse and guilt, Frank took himself out of town along the shore and went down to the sea at Nahoon mouth, walked out across the sand and stood as best he could at the water's edge staring out over the deep. It was usually the end of the day and in the dusk and from a distance you might have mistaken his outline for a marooned upright of a long vanished groyne. They had told him that the sea would return what it took when it was time, and so he waited. He thought it might come to him how he should take the next step, for their parents did not yet know that Harry was gone. Would it be better to tell them while he was still "missing", and then there could still be a chance, if you believed hard enough? Or was it better to wait until hope was pointless because death was certain?

He was in the throes of such reflection that night, like every night, as he lay awake on his bed. He thought he heard some shouting, no words just another sound emerging through the drone of the waves on the stony shore, then nothing, then again, then... then a sharp knocking on his door. It was daylight.

Sometime, while he was sleeping, his brother's body was washed up. The police came to his door at 7. At 10, after the identification, he was in the Post Office to send a telegram to his father. Around midday the hotel manager came to his room to tell him that his father was waiting for him on the telephone in his office.

The morning had been a blur. Frank was trembling as he went downstairs.

"Tell me this is some mistake, some mischief, something you've got wrong. Tell me... Tell me..."

Frank was not sure whether he was hearing incandescent rage or bottomless despair. The line was slow and noisy.

"Harry's gone, Father. I saw him 2 hours ago. I had to identify him. It was horrible. I don't know what to do."

"Why weren't you with him? You said you would stay with him. What have you done? What have you done?"

"I can't swim like he can. He just goes off. There's no point me swimming with him, I cannot hold him back."

"He was only 18. You lost him. You lost our youngest."

"Father, tell me what to do."

"Wait."

"They say they will bury him tomorrow."

"You wait and you repent...

"He must have a proper grave. Wait for me until I come."

"Father it will take you weeks and..."

The line went down. There was no call back, not that day, or the next, or at all.

2 weeks later Frank received a telegram:

EMBARK SS SAXON STHPTN 25 JUN ARR E LOND END JLY. INFORM HOTEL.

Why so long? The passage took weeks, but not that many, and there was no lack of steamers. Frank felt lost. He stumbled around aimlessly for several days, he sat on the sea shore, he hauled himself to the river quays, into the town, and struggled back down to the sea. He barely ate or drank. There was noise around him everywhere, the trippers at the beach, the constant movement of cargo boats in and out of the river, the clamour of loading and unloading on the docksides, traffic and trams on Oxford Street, round and round again and again, Esplanade, river and back down through town, but he might as well have been stumbling his way in circles on the endless empty veldt, the scraping of his shoe on the ground the only contact he felt with anything. No sense of time or of there having been anything before this, nor any hope that there would be anything after. He was moving and he was motionless with every step.

He turned over in his mind so many alternatives and put to himself so many questions, no, accusations - he could not avoid the blame which in the end turned to self-mockery with the scornful jibe that he did not have the stomach for the risk. Where Harry had preferred to swim - from the water's edge in front of the Beach Hotel - it was not an inviting sandy strand, but large slabs of flattish rock giving way in places to an uncomfortable stony shore with the restless ocean constantly harrassing. No firm comfortable footing, but a seabed quickly shelving, suiting well a strong confident swimmer like his brother who swam straight out to sea, exhilarated by the chill of deep water. Before, even when they were back in England, Frank's preference was always for an easy safe entry and calm water, and so now even more, he would demur when invited to join Harry's regular evening swim.

That evening had been one such - making an excuse of needing to check some material and then write some letters, he had got back to the Beach Hotel a little before sunset at 6. He looked down to the sea and was sure he saw Harry about 200 yards out and swimming parallel to the shore. It seemed a little choppy but not too much, and it was Friday, which meant there were people on the bank along the Esplanade and, apart from that, there was at least another two hours of daylight. So Frank went up to his room to read and to write a couple of letters. There was no agreement between the two of them that Harry would report when he came out of the water (though sometimes he did and then they would usually go along to the hotel bar for a drink), or that Frank would go down to the sea to make sure his brother had come back safely. So Frank never made a mental note to check at any particular time and in fact on this evening had fallen asleep. Suddenly woken by the loud banging on his door he was disorientated for several seconds. Thunderous thuds on hollow door panels in cavernous darkness. Coming round and staggering for support, at the same time scattering books and papers on the floor, he lurched to the door and grabbed at the handle, jerking it suddenly open and received a thump on his chest as Nobomi hammered again for entry.

Harry's girlfriend fell hard against him. He reeled back into the darkened room just as the silhouettes of the manager and his assistant blocked out the light from the corridor, which might at least have allowed his dulled senses to latch on to something that could bring order to the eruption. The girl was sobbing, the manager was serious and foreboding, the assistant was quickly edging round to try to dislodge Nobomi who was clinging desperately to his shirt.

In an imperious tone, which despite voicing an apology, seemed to contain a certain self-satisfaction, the manager delivered his dictum: "I must profusely apologise that you have been inconvenienced in this way, sir, and assure you that such things cannot normally happen in our hotel, but unfortunately the front door staff were engaged helping another guest when this, eh, girl, rushed past and seemingly found her way to your room. I cannot even contemplate how she might have known where to find you," (he paused), "but you may be confident that, if you appraise us of the details, you will not encounter any such discomfiting behaviour again."

With that, his assistant tried harder to dislodge Nobomi, but now the clinging was both ways and Frank countered, "Look, she's upset, she has come for help, she is my brother's girlfriend. Please leave us in peace so that I can find out what is wrong."

The manager righteously persisted: "Regrettably she is a native girl, Sir, and we have a policy..."

"Harry did not come back. A long time now. Must be drowned."

The wail of agony cut through the soulless banality. For a few moments there was a strangled silence behind the sobbing and then the muffled shuffling of the exit of manager and assistant. The door closed and darkness held the space once more. A kind of peace returned.

That night had been long. At some stage they walked together the short distance back to Harry's room in Fitzpatrick Road, which for a few months now had been home for Nobomi too. They sat on the bed until she had fallen asleep and then Frank left to return to the Beach Hotel. There he found himself an outcast, for the door was locked and no-one came to open it. He walked along the Esplanade, sat for a while on the bank staring out over the now becalmed ocean, and finally returned to Harry's.

Now the waiting, and the wondering.

Barbara

She never knew for certain how or when her father had lost his leg. As most children do, she had simply accepted what came from before she was born and had written it in to her idea of how life was, so that it was not something that ever came up for question. In the same way, the relatives were the relatives, and the fact that she once could have had one more uncle than anyone had told her about, would have seemed incomprehensible in her early years. That his name was Harry and that it all had something to do with South Africa - Harry and her father's leg, that is - she believed she only uncovered as an adult. But even then, and for the rest of her life, the picture was blurred and vague, strands of information, wisps and whispers. There had been mention of a bike accident and the Boer War and getting injured and from somewhere a black girl and a place called Matatiele, which she could never find on any map.

The father she knew was an engineer, skilled enough, her mother had told her, to have designed and made his own prosthetic leg, more than one in fact because he had modified and improved his own original drawings, and all that when there were no specialist materials or workshops. And so she knew her father as a skilful man and a determined man - not for him the limited life of the soldiers who returned limbless from Crimea or the Boer War or the First World War, for he was a professional and also a factory manager of some acclaim, being awarded successive substantial payments for his innovations. And all this was important for her as the eldest, because it meant the family lived in a large company-funded house which set her apart from her peers in the industrial environs of Lancashire.

She was aware of being apart; socially apart, for her father was a boss, geographically apart for, wherever people might have imagined the family had come from, it was certainly not from Lancashire, and there was something else, something which had a significance she did not know until much later. It was in the genes: her mother's father had been Norwegian. She was told he had died at sea and she could not remember ever meeting him, the sole reminder left of her forebear being the remarks she could still recall from visitors when she was very young that "yes, she does look a little bit Scandinavian".

But if there were traces of Scandinavian in her appearance, none of the social informality we now associate with those countries found fertile ground in the rather staid home setting in which she grew up. Somehow the detached surveillance of the (now deceased) Richard-Symons (paternal grandfather), though he had lived at the other end of the country, pervaded the comfortable conditions at Windmill Hill. The louche young man that once had been her grandfather had yielded to the demands of professional practice (as well as the needs of a large family) and metamorphosed into an ordered, correct and conventional head of the family. Whatever might have been the effect of later events, the model of family life in which her own father grew up was traditional and patriarchal. So it was likely that the potential for an easy-going, even insouciant, approach to life in Barbara had been stifled by the formalities of this most English home environment. Right through her childhood she was a model of respectable offspring, and then too right through those years of dutiful caring and self-abnegation, until the War finally released her into adulthood.

Already 22 when the second war was declared, but with little close contact outside her family, its impact was bewildering in its divergent effects. The orderliness of everyday life changed little at first, once she had learnt to parry a mother's obsession with stockpiling, carried over from "the last time"; but she noticed her own growing sense of unpreparedness and an anxiety that what had seemed so solid no longer felt assured. The counterpoint was the dawning of a kind of freedom, her world no longer solely bounded by family expectations, the unspoken norms being progressively overridden in these new circumstances, where the only safe currency was self-sufficiency.

But the displacement of constraining conventions in the face of unpredictable peril brought an almost bipolar vacillation of her emotions, and a confusing perception of her needs. She was steady and business-like by nature, but in the face of uncertainty needed a solid base. She married Norman, 10 years older, though no-one remarked on the age difference of course because he fitted so well, and in him she found her solid ground.

But the book was not closed.

the third room

It is not in the nature of human beings to stand still. It is very rare that the mind does not eventually start to notice differences, minuscule changes creating unexpected contrasts, barely perceptible shifts, this, even when the predominant sense is one of emptiness, debilitation and hopeless failure. Like the boxer knocked to the floor who struggles to his feet just before the end of the count, the brain registers one infinitesimal deviation from its unconscious assumption of desolation. It would be that way with Frank in the end, but not quite yet. His aimless shamblings continued for several days.

People began to be used to seeing him, because although his times of passing were not always the same each day, his route changed little. It always included the dockside, where he expected to meet his father in due course, and he usually came back to the Esplanade down Fitzpatrick Road. Perhaps neither were really choices as much as sub-conscious inevitability. In a sense they were the only two physical points of reference that he registered now, since both were markers, the one from the world he must rejoin, the other in the new world he had scarcely embraced. In truth he had done little to put down roots in this new world. But here was the source of one of the first differences which he noticed.

White Cat

The day before the telegram from his father arrived and 13 days after he had identified Harry at the hospital, he was walking again down Fitzpatrick Road past the unkempt entrance of the building which contained Harry's room. He was later than usual, so it was almost dark and the same light glimmered through the window beside the door as on that night when he had brought Nobomi home. It came into his mind that unlike himself, and despite his having been around for only a short time, Harry *had* started to put down roots. From the beginning he had insisted on somewhere separate to live. He had refused the Beach Hotel (a bit expensive for their circumstances, but Frank would have paid) and insisted on finding these down at heel lodgings which would have caused consternation for their parents. And then within a few short weeks he had a girlfriend, and not just that but a native girl. That of course was just like Harry - no concern for norms or risks, which are always an unknown for an incomer in a new environment and which in this case were many and multifarious. Their family was British and distinctly English, but would not have thought themselves in any way imperialist in their attitudes. Nevertheless, who in the Cape would not register that their country was in the process of constructing an arrangement designed to cement its control, political but more importantly economic, over a vast area, with a population composed of many and sundry nationalities and ethnic origins, and where the more numerous native population would be used as agents of their own economic exploitation? Such and more was the analysis which Frank would apply to their situation. But pragmatic not prejudiced. If you had heard him express this you would have realised that prejudice was nowhere in view. His brother, though, would not even have seen the relevance of such observations, even if some would say he put it there, even by ignoring it. Typical of Harry was his very nonchalance over his native girlfriend - a matter which the hotel manager "regretted" and for which he had "a policy". Frank knew his brother's unconcerned approach to life was not in his own nature, but yet a small part of him envied it, might just emulate it even, as he felt his anxiety rising at the shadows appearing in the wings.

It came as no surprise to Frank to find the manager of the Beach Hotel waiting for him one evening when he arrived back, with the request, no, demand, that he find somewhere different to stay. "You understand, Sir, I am sure, that we are promoting our hotel as a restful and agreeable establishment for that part of our country's people who are able to appreciate our taste and ambience. You, being a man of, eh, business, would likely be better served in a more lively, perhaps stimulating setting. I will of course be pleased to provide you with a couple of possible places which might be more fitting. We are coming to our peak with holiday visitors and so I would ask for your prompt attention to the matter. Shall we say to complete arrangements by the day after tomorrow?"

"You are a snob, sir", replied Frank.

And there was the second difference, which without warning came to his attention. He had said this without hesitation and without anxiety and he still felt completely unflustered, he could almost say unconcerned, yes, that was how he felt, unconcerned.

The next day he moved into his brother's room, which for some reason he had not cleared and had continued to pay the rent for. This probably had to do with Nobomi and wanting to do the right thing, but he had not even tried to rationalise the decision. Nobomi, he knew, was somehow a resident in one of the 'concentration camps', which was a descriptive term for the British policy of holding and gathering the Boer farmers and sundry natives (mainly women and children) populating different areas of Cape Colony, to force them back into the hinterland where they could be more effectively contained and administered. There was one such camp in East London, whose residents were principally Dutch or Germanic immigrants, but also had native Africans in smaller numbers. The natives, however, appeared to be much more of a floating population and seemed to go in and out of the place at their own inclination, chiefly because of the possibility of food.

Nobomi, though still admitted to the camp, had been reluctant to leave Fitzpatrick Road. Often she still stayed overnight. Frank asked no questions and the arrangement between them was clear, that this came from his affection for his brother. (Sometimes, though, he caught himself wondering if it was not as much from the guilt he felt on his brother's behalf.)

Accordingly she slept on the floor and he acquired another mattress for this purpose. When she was there in the evening she cooked for both of them, but there was no obligation and no commitment.

"I'm pregnant," said Nobomi a few days after he had moved in.

He looked up quickly and caught her gaze before she lowered her eyes. "Harry? You know?"

"Before, no. Now, yes. I have no man."

"You know for certain?"

She looked across to him again steadily and sincerely. "I know."

His dead brother's unborn child. The mother. Himself.

Suddenly the rest of the world emptied, like a stage where the crowd in the scene quickly disperses and the spotlights narrow their beams to light just the players centre stage. They were centre stage. And there was no script. For what seemed like ages he could find no words.

"Did Harry know?"

A long pause, then "Yes."

Who are the people we think we know?

For any less adept thinker, the full import of that one "Yes" would have taken time to surface. But Frank was assailed by a torrent of thoughts, fears and questions in an instant. What came first was a feeling of betrayal on several levels, brother not talking to brother, deprived of a chance to help, no sense of male chivalry, betrayal even of that aspect of him that Frank was seeking now to emulate, for surely the unconcerned Harry would not have needed to deliberately risk, perhaps even take, his life. "Did I really just think that?" Who was the brother who could leave this girl who held a part of him inside her? How desperately Frank now felt he was floundering - no knowledge or skill that could help him, nothing he could draw on that made him even adequate. Yet he could not walk away from this native girl who would have a child which would not be seen as 'pure' amongst her own. And would be one of *his* own. But still no intuition came with an answer. The engineer he was could not design a mechanism with an outcome for this. Not this challenge. Not this time.

No, he could not walk away. The part of Harry which he was trying to be would be untroubled by the difficulties and the odds against him, and would simply manage. Walking away would not have been part of any solution.

"But Harry, that's what you've done!" Inside he was screaming at his brother.

And for the Frank from before, the Frank who would be an engineer, to not find a solution could never be an option; that Frank was ordered, in a world that must have order, a world also in which honour and chivalry were the highest order, but how to reconcile chivalry for this girl with duty owed to a patriarchal family from the old country?

Eventually, he drew his chair across the tiny room until he could be directly opposite Nobomi who was sitting on the bed. He held out his hands, elbows resting on his knees, palms upwards. She hesitated. But this was not any exploratory prurient gesture. She looked at him and he at her and perhaps he saw the faintest easing of the tension in her face as she placed her hands palms down on his.

"I will not leave you alone," he said.

~~~

Letter from Barbara to Peter 4th June 1948

Dear Peter,

Thank you for your reply. Of course it was not what I wanted to hear, but it was what I needed to hear. Funny how someone else tells you what you know you are telling yourself but refusing to listen to. Yes, I should not set any store by this and I should not burn any bridges. I can say that now, here in my protective nest in English suburbia.

But what if he writes? He hasn't yet. At least I haven't got it if he has. OK, I think I can manage to go on waiting until it comes, if it's going to.

But strange as it may seem, that was not quite what I wanted to write about. You know how I am fascinated by old family things and previous generations. And names. Parents do funny things naming their children. In some cultures children are named after objects or animals or how they came to be born or gods to bless them, it's especially like that in Africa. That's a thought, I haven't looked at how they name children in India. But over here we seem to give children at least one name that comes from a forebear. (Surely that causes problems sometimes because there must be two sets of forebears, never mind how many generations do you go back?)

I don't think the female side gets the exposure they are due in most families' histories, either documented or anecdotal. It seems very unfair, because after all they are at least fifty per cent responsible, never mind liable (and some would say more, in terms of pain and risk) for the continuation of the family line, which always first of all seems to mean the male family line - very much the male line in ours, which I think has always been quite patriarchal. Maybe that's my imagination, perhaps it hasn't been any worse than most over the years. It's just that the women's side doesn't seem to get recognised like the men's. They are always the ones who "are married" not the ones who do the marrying. You know our family has some wonderful women's names too. There was a Fanny Hester <u>and</u> a Fanny Esther. There have been Beatrice's and Louisa's and then of course our mother, who wasn't really Mollie as everybody called her, but Ada Florence. (Between you and me I'm not surprised she preferred to live as Mollie.)

Anyway, I'm going to make it my contribution to our family history to highlight the lives of the women, wives <u>and</u> daughters (because the daughters usually go off and get lost on someone else's family tree of course).

I suppose it's not surprising it all feels a bit patriarchal, because I noticed that there were more boys than girls in each generation. Until you get to our father. In his generation there were 3 of each. But we didn't know that until a couple of years ago, did we? I still keep forgetting his name, the lost brother, but that meant they were equal, boys and girls. For those 3 girls, though, a different kind of inequality. None of them got married. Their's was the generation of the First War. Do you think that was why? Some people say there weren't enough men afterwards. So that must have rather stunted the line, you might say. As for our lost uncle, the one that seems to have drowned in South Africa, did he start a family before that happened, do you think? Is there a whole other line we don't know about?

All this talk about children. I've got to own up again. I spent a lot of time trying to work things out, work me out I mean and where I really am and what was going on that I even sat down at that table in the Pump Rooms. Seeing myself doing it in my mind, I can still hardly believe it's me.

Anyway, my conclusion is that it's about children. You've probably guessed that side of things isn't working for us, me and Norman. If you haven't guessed, mother has, because she keeps asking, but I can't talk to her. It's not working but not because it doesn't get the chance, there's plenty of chance for it to work, but something's wrong. We don't know what.

We've been for examinations, both of us, but nobody seems able to tell us anything for definite. To be honest I think the hospitals are still struggling from the war. Certainly they don't have enough staff and people keep getting moved around, you never see the same person twice. There's supposed to be some way to do it artificially (fertilisation they call it), which is being experimented with in America, but what they fall back on here is psycho-analysis. "It's in the mind". You hear that a lot.

But I'm not meaning to talk about nitty-gritty, I'm explaining me, because I think this has something to do with the turmoil my mind's been in. I want children (or at least one, I don't want our grandfather's 6 or even our mother's 4), and I want to give myself the best chance. That's it. Simple as that. Nothing to do with me and Norman, we get on very well. He's solid and I need solid. But I also seem to need children.

Now I'm going to stop. But after our last letters I thought you should know, now that I've worked it out. You don't have to feel sorry for me. Kindly brotherly interest will be fine. But

I feel better knowing what it is. And if Hugh doesn't write, that's an end of it.

Your loving sister,

Barbara

the lens of time

Author's journal 8th December 2021

How interesting that wherever we look and whatever we look at the image we get is complete. Not complete in the sense that we can see everything that could possibly in some circumstance be seen, but that what we do see is a whole picture. Our brain is masterful at filling in the gaps which time or distance render indecipherable. Like the separate frames of a film which miraculously become a continuous flow of moving imagery. Like the form of the tree, which really is hundreds of thousands of small leaf shapes hanging from an impressive matrix of branches and trunk, but somehow from our distance is a tree. Convenient of course because we can't handle all the data at once. But it's still all there - the lens captures everything.

So what happens to the bits we don't 'see'? Surely they're still around somewhere, doing something?

Nobomi

Nobomi was a Xhosa, the second largest native group in Southern Africa. Their traditional homeland is the Eastern Cape, the part of Cape Colony in which is sited East London, stretching from the Indian Ocean out across the hilly hinterland which rises towards the Winterberg then the Drakensberg, mountain ranges 100 miles and more inland. It is a terrain of grass-covered uplands, scattered randomly with scrub bush and trees, and dense forest tracking the river valleys. Despite its harshness and the frequent discomforts of its climate, there is a serenity about the landscape, which belies the three significant conflicts the area witnessed in the half century before Harry's death, the last, the second Boer War, only ending formally little more than a month after he drowned.

Nobomi was AmaMfengu and so she was an embodiment of the Xhosa tradition of assimilating those who accepted their culture and adopted their customs. For hundreds of years now, identification as Xhosa had been political as much as ethnic. AmaMfengu, the wanderers, were the latest in a long line of tribal groups that fate or conflict had brought into the Xhosa people. It was not any kind of associate membership and more than merely residency, rather it was an interconnection which became a filial link.

Nobomi's family were of the Bhele people and had lived on the Savannah well inland in the northern part of Eastern Cape bordering the Zulu lands of Natal. An area of wide open plains fringed with craggy mountain ranges and dotted with the clusters of thatched round houses of a people whose livelihood came from cattle and meagre crops. But though the living was poor the management of the common livelihood gave stability to a social structure which was collaborative and which, with the landscape, traced the pathway from the ancestors, leading on through each generation, as they themselves became ancestors.

Nobomi was born in 1885, in the same year as Harry; she in a scattered village of native farmsteads known as Matatiele, each family area unfenced but tending its own space of around 50 yards diameter; he in a comfortable Georgian terrace house close to the centre of a busy commercial port. Her people were of the Bantu ethnic grouping and in the conduct of their personal lives held to *ubuntu*, the belief that each person is only complete as who they are if the person alongside can also be who they are.

Thirty or so years earlier her clan had been the victims of Zulu territorial expansion and the Mfecane wars, which were a part of the evolution, over half a millenium, of southern Africa into a modern South Africa, a transformation from the empty pastoral home of bushmen into an uneasy coalition of economic political ethnic and linguistic interests and diversity. Forced out by the conflict, with their people, Nobomi's family had trekked west and south, moving into the

Eastern Cape and the traditional lands of the Xhosa tribes. Anthropologists would say that much was already shared by the different peoples of the Bantu nations, but her family's tribal group adopted the customs and culture of the Xhosa and became known as the Wanderers, the AmaMfengu.

Harry was the youngest of six children born to Richard-Symons and his wife Fanny-Esther. The family was well-established, his father a printer and publisher.

Nobomi was the youngest of three girls born to Nyaniso and his wife Thozoma. When she was 10 she remembers her mother telling her about her father's anxiety because he could not perform a true *imbeleko* at her birth and bury her cord in ancestral grounds, for they had settled there in Matatiele and could no longer return to their traditional home. He worried that this would rob her of her roots and could mean that she would be a wanderer all her life.

She was 15 when she left the family home. She had been a good pupil at the mission school in Matatiele and had spent a year after this living away in order to go to school in Mthatha. Then from 13 she had worked in the house and on the farm, but she could see the strain her father bore from being the only man in their household of limited means and without the physical help of a son. It was worse because the wider family were too far away to help, and anyway her father had only two brothers and each of these had more children than Nyaniso and Thozoma. She had not been sure why it should be for her to leave rather than her eldest sister, but maybe it was right because she was younger and was of less value. Did she believe her father's fears about her incomplete birth rituals? It shouldn't worry her, she knew, because the ritual introduction to the ancestors could be completed at any time, and it was only that in her case it would never be in the ancestors' land. And his concern for her never finding the place for her life and always being a wanderer? Right now, at least, that did not concern her. She had been taught that it was Xhosa custom to accept as Xhosa anyone who followed their culture and practices and her family had felt accepted in Matatiele for many years now. Why would she not be accepted by others of her people? She only knew herself as AmaMfengu Xhosa.

She was sure that it was good that she chose to leave now, for she had the confidence of youth, and this might falter in even another year or so. But still, as she walked away, it was as if there were two separate parts of her; the physical part, her body, which she could make act as if nothing special was happening and stride out with her head held high; and the part inside which was almost quivering, sometimes with excitement, but more often with apprehension, about what might lie round the next bend on the track.

Nobomi headed first for Mthatha. She had been told this route was the safest way south and she had walked it 2 years before to go to school there. There was the best chance of being able to find food in Xhosa settlements and the least possibility of needing to approach Burgher farms, where there was always a risk of being forcibly held as a worker. Mthatha, also, was big enough to have possibilities for work amongst her own kind and the added activity and jobs which came from it being a British military post. She had little idea about distance or travelling time and even if someone had given her that information it would have meant little to her. In fact, even if she had been able to find the most direct tracks and roads, it was a distance of over 120 miles, which in any circumstances she could not have covered in less than ten days.

~~~

Nobomi arrived at Mthatha ten weeks later.

The following year she came to East London.

conversations...1

Letter from Hugh to Barbara 1st June 1948

Dear Barbara

I'm sorry this has been so long coming. I can imagine what might have been going through your mind - some Rupert after a bit of soul-comfort practicing his chat-up lines, a few hours to kill, that sort of thing. I wouldn't blame you, so I hope you'll believe me when I tell you it wasn't anything like that. No, I arrived back and the unit was in the process of moving base. We are just outside the city on the Russian side of the British area, but we are being moved closer to the boundary between us and the Russians because there's concern they might be trying to create a bigger buffer, or at least that would be the pretext. In reality, we have a fairly large area of good agricultural land which they want to acquire, because they are trying to control as much of the food (and oil) supply as they can. They already have most of it. (I say "we have..."

but in the end the aim of the occupation is to create a viable Austrian state, which can exist and govern itself. The Occupation is not to carry on when that is done.)

There's all sorts of mistrust here, because the War has left some parts of Austrian society divided against other parts, never mind the complete dissolution of any semblance of consensual political system, plus the destruction of infrastructure and massive amounts of housing. Vienna itself is under a joint command with the Yanks the Russkis the Brits and the Frogs taking it in turns to manage the show. No problems there then! Hmm. Anyway more significant for me is that I am likely going to be moved into some sort of 'liaison' role - which you will probably guess is a euphemism - and transfer into that central command in the city. I don't know yet what that might mean in terms of the possibility of writing out, because that sort of thing is pretty closely monitored.

But all that wasn't really what I was writing about. I really just wanted to say how much I appreciated your company the day before I was returning. It was so good to have a breath of life outside the 'battle zone'. No, it's not quite a battle zone - I try to tell myself that I should think of it as peace-keeping and mediation, in order to keep my attitude constructive, but battle zone is my slang because that's what it feels like sometimes and the feeling builds up well before I actually get back. So thanks for some human contact which wasn't mates, or command, or squaddies, or even family!

I've got to be careful here. I could easily drift into loads of stuff about how miserable my lot is and touting for sympathy and using you as a crutch, and that might seem like I'm trying to set myself up for a warm bed when I finally get out of this hell-hole.

But I'm honestly not doing any of that. I just want to say how sweet you were to me and how our few hours together meant so much. Oh, and I hope your slashed tyre wasn't too much of an inconvenience! And if by any chance our correspondence were to be continued, I would tell you a bit about myself and perhaps you would tell me about yourself too. But right now, this is just me saying "thank you".

Appreciatively yours,
Hugh

ps. just in case you want to, to write to me you must address the envelope as follows:

4574055 LT. WINTERS
FSS VIENNA
BFPO 5260

~~~

<u>Letter from Barbara to Hugh 13th June 1948</u>

Dear Hugh

I was pleased and confused to receive your letter. It is these times we are living through I think. Just when it seems like I might at last be getting back to a normal existence again... and then something happens which feels like it belongs to the world of chaos and confusion. I say getting back to normal, but that's a very selfish view I know, because it's nowhere near normal for those poor people around you where you are. I try to imagine what it must be like, so many families and so few places left to make a home, children having to sleep in the ruins.

No I can't do this, I have a job and a home.

I'm not making much sense, am I?

I have a job and a home and I am safe. But I need to breathe. Perhaps that was what the afternoon in Bath gave me - somewhere to breathe. Because I did feel better. And the strangest thing - home had started to feel like a leaden weight, claustrophobic, and I know it affected how I was with Norman, everything becoming a dull endless repetition - but when I got back in after leaving you (once I stopped fretting about where I was going to get a new front tyre - we do still have shortages you know) I looked round the sitting room and I thought I'd made a good job of it with the curtains and the flowers and I smiled at the cooker which I had given a good clean the day before and I even got the good china down for us to have a cup of tea and I <u>wanted</u> to do it for Norman.

And now I'm completely confused.

I must not do this. I must not drag you down with my bewilderment. You need all your wits about you for the incredible job you are doing. I must not take up your time, you're such a darling. God, what have I just said? I must go, I don't know what's going to happen.

Yours sincerely,

Barbara

Letter from Hugh to Barbara 20th June 1948

Dear Barbara

Please don't trouble yourself or get distressed. The last thing I want is to disturb your life, but now I am wondering whether I am being selfish myself in enjoying our contact even just by letter. It doesn't seem right to enjoy something which is getting you perplexed.

I'm not going to say any more now. I was handed your letter just half an hour ago and I wanted you to know that I had got it and read it and just want the best for you and I will write very shortly when I am in slightly more peaceful surroundings and have cleared my head of the day's clutter.

With my sincere good wishes,
Hugh

~~~

On 2nd July 1900 Nobomi walked into the Post Office in Oxford Street, East London to send a communication to her family saying that she was safe and thought she would stay in this place for a time. Behind the counter was a clerk, a young Englishman - she thought that apart from his hair and the colour of his skin he could have been one of her cousins, not at all what she expected. He looked up.

"Who are you?" she asked

"Harry"

"No not your name. Who? I want someone who can send a message to my family."

"I am the telegraph clerk. I can do that. Where are your family?"

"They are in Matatiele. It is beyond Mthatha."

"Can you tell me what direction and how far beyond Mthatha?"

"Below the mountains of Basotho."

"That could be as far as this on the other side of Mthatha."

"I think it is. It took me several weeks to walk from my family home to Mthatha. Can you send a letter there?"

"You are a long long way from your home."

"I am looking for a home. I am AmaMfengu."

"I could telegraph your message to Mthatha, there is a military post there, and I could ask them to write your message down and give it to the next person travelling towards the mountains. But it might take several weeks to arrive."

"I only have a little money."

"There is no rate to deliver that far, but if you pay me the amount to telegraph to Mthatha I will ask the clerk there to pass it on and I will tell him the charge is paid."

"How much?"

"That depends on what you write. You can write it down here and I will tell you."

He handed her the form and Nobomi wrote:

Molo Mama nawe Tata nawe oodade, ndiyanibulisa nani sisi. Ndiyanibhalela ukuze ndinazise ukuba ndiphilile. NdiseMonti, yidolophu engakulwandlwe olukhulu, yaye ndiza kukhe ndihlale khona ukuze ndibone ukuba andinakuyenza ikhaya na. Ndiza kuphinda ndinibhalele. Ndiyanithanda. NguNobomi.

"There, can you read it?"

"I can read the letters to send them on the wire, but I don't know what it means."

"It means this: My dear Mama and Papa and sisters, I am writing to say I am well. I am in East London, which is by the big sea, and I am going to see if I can live here so that it can be my home. I will write again. I love you. Nobomi."

"It is quite long. But let me work out how much it will be."

Harry sat down, lifted a dog-eared book out of the desk, searched for a page, then took the message and studied it. To Nobomi he appeared to be counting every letter and then he looked at his book, took another piece of paper and wrote what seemed to be calculations. Then he put down his pencil and stared at the message for a long time before standing up to speak to her again.

"I cannot find the correct rate for sending this to Mthatha," and he looked around as if to check there was no-one else in the office, "I will just send it."

"How much?"

"Nothing."

"Why?"

Harry looked down at the message. He was thinking. He knew why, but he did not dare to say.

"You are a long long way from home." Then, recovering himself: "I will send it later in the morning, when we do the despatches. If you want to come back in the afternoon, Miss Nobomi, I will be able to tell you it has gone."

Nobomi looked at him and smiled her thank you, then turned and walked slowly to the door.

Miss Nobomi? Nobody had ever called her that before.

~~~

Letter from Hugh to Barbara 20th June 1948

Dear Barbara

It is now quite late, but it's Sunday tomorrow and I am relieved for the day, so I can stay in bed. Doesn't often happen, so you have to take advantage.

There are lots of things I want to say, but few things I feel I should, or even know how to say. Like I said this morning, I feel selfish in even taking your time by writing. I would like to be stronger and tell myself that even though you gave me your attention and wrote back to me, that doesn't give me the right to let you do it just because it's helping me. Oh listen to me! I sound like I'm talking to some little girl. I hope you'll forgive me if I sound patronising. Little girl? I don't think so. You didn't tell me what you did in the War, but I don't think you sat at home knitting!

conversations...1

This may sound silly, but for me it doesn't seem to be about <u>what</u> I say. I could talk about anything, say anything (not make things up I don't mean), it's just the talking (writing) and knowing that someone is listening. Yes, that's what was so good about our afternoon in the Pump Rooms, it didn't matter what we talked about, it was just being interested in each other and listening and where that took us.

I'm going a long way round trying to say I would really like it if we could 'talk' by letter like this, just because you are a person I find interesting and, I think, I am a person you find interesting. We will both be broadening our view of the world and learning things we didn't know, just for the hell of it. As a way in, we could start with trivial things, things from long ago which don't matter, like where we were born and parents and siblings and things and school, and just see where it goes. What do you think? I won't put anything about me yet, in case you want to stop this here. But that's not pushing you into starting off with something.

You could write back and just say YES, and then I'll go first. What do you think?

Your friend,

Hugh

~~~

Nobomi went back to the Post Office in the middle of the afternoon. She walked in. Again it was deserted except for the man behind the counter, but he was not Harry. She was about to turn and leave again when he looked up and caught her eye. Uncertainly she walked across to the counter.

"Can I help you?"

But no words came.

"Oh, you are the girl this morning Harry told me about. He was sent out on a delivery to Duncan and might not be back before we close. But he left this for you." The man handed her a brown envelope.

"Thank you." She took it and she wanted to run, but that might not be right. With great difficulty she walked fairly steadily to the door, but once outside made a bolt for the nearest alley as fast as she could.

In the envelope was a type-written message on official-looking paper:

conversations...1

Dear Miss Nobomi,

I am sorry that I cannot tell you this personally, but I confirm that I have sent your message to Mthatha and asked them to give it to the first person who is going towards Matatiele. As I said, I think it will take several weeks to arrive, but I am sure that it will be good news for your family.

I understand what it is like to be a long way from home, I am also a long way from home, and I hope that you will find people to help you in East London. If our service, or even I myself, can do anything to help you settle here, it would be a pleasure to do this. You may contact me at 45 Fitzpatrick Road, or of course you can come to the Post Office at any time it is open.

Most faithfully yours,

Harry Cole (Post Office Clerk)

Miss Nobomi. There it was again. Nobomi had heard about white people - there were white people in charge of the Mission schools - and she had seen pictures in school - but until she had been walking for a few days on her way to Mthatha, she had never had to talk to white people she did not know. And that first meeting had not been good, for a Burgher's family had tried to hold her on their farm to do domestic work and she had had to escape in the middle of the night. She had decided to only approach her own people after that. But now she was in a big town in the rest of the world, and who was this white boy who was a long way from home as well and she had smiled at? And he called her **Miss** Nobomi. But why didn't he smile back?

~~~

Letter from Barbara to Hugh 29th June 1948

Dear Hugh

YES

Barbara

Letter from Hugh to Barbara 1st July 1948

Dear Barbara

Well I asked for it I suppose. You don't mind putting a chap on the spot, do you? Right, where shall I start?

I have a sister called Sophie. Despite sounding like a southerner I was born in Sheffield. My father teaches economics at the University and my mother is a secretary. So despite being the country's dirtiest city (especially when you include the east side and all the steel works and the Rother valley) we are horribly middle class and the family home is on the pretty side of town where it goes up towards the Peak District. Did a lot of walking up there in my teens. Buses and trains were good for getting to starting places to get up onto the fells. I went to the local primary school, but, as you probably guessed not the secondary. I was sent away "down south". Then I went to Bristol University and joined up straight after that. That was when the war was on the horizon, even though there was all the denial going on. I'd been brought up in the patriotism mould, so I thought I could do the Army thing into my early 30s and reach a decent rank, which would stand me in good stead in civvy street. In fact I'm pretty much decided this is my last commission, so the plan is more or less in place. You know I told you I like classical music and opera. Well, I'm hoping that if this is my last commission, they'll finish the re-building of the Vienna State Opera before I have to leave, so that I can go to something there - they finally decided to make it like the original. But I don't see it happening. It was supposed to be 1949, also conveniently an election year, a symbolic boost to morale, but I can't see it, there's too much politics here. Though this is one altruistic thing the Russians are interested in. I'm not sure whether that will help or not, but I don't think I really go along with spending so much on an arts *project until you've got people off the streets into proper housing.*

I'm getting on my soapbox again. But perhaps that's enough for this time. Let's do the chatty stuff, the casual exchanging ideas bit. But I don't mind you telling me what you would like to know. And whether you mind me drifting into the heavier things. That's what feels so isolating here. The Army doesn't do philosophy clubs and interest groups like university! And I'm not sure it would work if they did - people are very conscious of appearance and how they come across.

OK, over to you.
All good wishes and happiness,
Hugh

~~~

On 14th July around 4 in the morning, there was a knock on the door of Harry's room at 45 Fitzpatrick Road. It was a Saturday. The room opened onto an external corridor to which anyone could gain access from the road, but in the five months he had been living there he had never had an unexpected caller, let alone in the middle of the night. He stumbled out of bed and across the room, but then he paused with his hand on the door lock.

conversations...1

"Who is it?"

"Miss Nobomi."

Flustered, he opened the door to her, but this was not the composed Nobomi who had walked up to him at the Post Office counter. The person he saw was dishevelled, tear-streaked, propping herself against the wall; her white dress was dirty and torn and her head and neck and arms were devoid of any of the jewellery which seemed to be essential for the black women he had seen. He held out his arms, then hesitated - might that seem like an incorrect advance? - but she fell forward against him and he supported her across the room to lay her down on the bed. He went back to close the door and when he turned he found her on her side with knees drawn up to her bowed head and sobbing, her whole body heaving and shuddering.

Neither his schooling, his friends, his brothers, certainly not his father, not any of these had prepared him for what to do with a distraught hysterical girl from a culture he knew nothing of in a dingy bed-sit 10,000 miles from home. He pulled the chair across to the bed and sat there, his hands trembling, not being sure whether he should touch her or try to hold her or what words might help. In the end he offered his handkerchief, and waited. He had heard his mother upset (though not like this) and he recognised a woman's crying, but this felt like something different, heaving sobs interspersed by wailing and then screamed words, which meant nothing to him.

He was surprised how, in spite of the hour, he felt completely awake, alert even, and acutely perturbed by this girl, who must be about his age, and must feel so alone. No-one should have to feel alone. Gradually, very gradually, her sobbing subsided. In the silence now came through the distant sound of the ocean waves breaking on the rocky shore. Their steady pulse was comforting and the stillness behind it brought peace.

Nobomi had moved onto her back and stretched out her legs. She held out her arm to him - "please" - and he helped her to sit up on the side of the bed. He was taken aback, but relieved, very relieved, at her recovery.

After a few moments: "There was nowhere else to go. Please don't make me leave."

"I do not want you to leave." He was surprised at the request.

Now a long pause. Harry brought a cover to put round her shoulders and went across and lit the cooker to prepare a drink.

Sitting on the bed still, she warmed her hands around the mug. She drank slowly bowing her head between each sip. Once finished she handed him the mug - "Thank you" - and continued to sit head bowed, hands clasped in front on her lap.

"They were my tribe and they gave me a room."...

"I do not understand the big town."... "Where my family live there are bad people too, but we know who they are or what they look like."... "Here I don't know, I cannot tell."

Again a long pause. The sound of the ocean stole through the silence. Harry sat and waited.

"I think I am spoiled. They came while I was asleep. I did not hear them coming. I could not escape. I could not fight them."... "Now I am spoiled."... "Please don't make me leave."

"I will not make you leave."

Another pause, then head bowed still. "Can I sleep now, please?"

"For as long as you need."

Nobomi sank back and lay out on the bed. Harry covered her with a blanket and lay down himself on what passed for a sofa on the other side of the room. Had he done what he should? What would his father think? No, more important, what would his mother think?

He listened to the beat of the ocean waves. Then he noticed it was not silence behind. There was the soft sound of her breathing. Nobomi. What does that mean? Nobomi.

That was the last question before he slept.

~~~

Letter from Barbara to Hugh 15th July 1948

Dear Hugh

Thank you for your letter. I go up and down, no forwards and backwards, so I replied YES like you said, but not writing anything else was a bit of an opt out. You of course keep to the bargain and write something like you suggested and that put me on the spot. So I've been thinking about it and putting it off for a bit.

I'm not going to do the biography stuff. Except to say you're Yorkshire and I'm Lancastrian. Well, that was where I was born, we came south when I was just 5, so I don't really feel as if I'm from Lancashire. And I think the family would consider they were southerners.

I suppose it's down to the War, not just our war but any war. For almost 5 years being alive was such an uncertain thing so it was just a case of 'what's happening now?' What you have today you might not have tomorrow, so don't treasure anything. Tomorrow might not happen, so don't plan anything. You took what you could, enjoyed what you could (if you were that lucky), when you could, because life might be gone tomorrow. But if you take the God perspective, the view from on high - incidentally I am not religious, despite almost ending up as the step-daughter of the Bishop of Oxford - but if you take the God perspective, looking down that is, it must be the whole panoply of living things that matter, Life with a capital 'L' in other words, and that means dying <u>has</u> to be going on all the time, as well as things being born. And here <u>we</u> are, we worry about dying as if we <u>individually</u> are important, instead of simply being significant just as part of Life as a whole (with a capital 'L'). It's a kind of play and you can't die without having lived but you can't live without dying. Things keep going round. Isn't that in the Bible somewhere? A time to be born and a time to die, a time of war and a time of peace, a time to mourn and a time to dance. But this play never ends and in a way neither do we, because we produce new people and

...

Sorry I had to take a break there. I didn't see that coming.

That's all a bit heavy isn't it, but I'm afraid that's me at the moment. It will probably scare you off. I am sorry if my amateur philosophy sounds rather flippant, because you are still living with the real aftermath of the War, whereas we just have to put up with a few shortages and streets with disappeared buildings.

I am a bit preoccupied with 'Life' at the moment and how it is going to work, in this world now which is so totally different to the one before. Not just the things you can feel, like shortages, or what you can see, like bomb-sites, but what you can't see like people's attitudes and ideas and expectations, and how to behave. And families.

I've got a brother, Peter. He was in the army in India during the War and is still there because he moved over to running a tea plantation. It suits him, but he doesn't know how much longer he will be able to stay following independence. But he was always someone who lived life as it came, no expectations, no recriminations, take what's there because it's there and because it's all part of the play. We exchange letters from time to time. First impressions, you are somewhere between the two of us. Our family has had a few oddball characters. There was a granduncle - Granduncle William - who was lost in the African jungle somewhere, the story was he went off to marry the "black queen"! That much was in the papers, but they never said whether he found her. And then there was an uncle we never saw and my father wouldn't talk about, Harry was his name, and he went to South Africa and was drowned, but some story about a black girl and a child. I could write to Aunt Louie and see if she will tell me something more about him. Sorry, I'm thinking aloud.

Well, I hope this hasn't been a total disaster for someone looking for a friendly word, and I hope things are going ok on the ground for you. I try to imagine what your part of the world looks like, but I don't think I get very close.

Good wishes and best regards,
Barbara

~~~

Nobomi was still sleeping when Harry got up at 7. For some reason, which he couldn't understand, he had to check she was breathing, so he went over to the bed and was relieved to see that she was. He sat down at the table and had his usual breakfast of two slices of bread and mug of tea. Being a Saturday he had to go to work, though only until midday this week. He wrote her a note before leaving, making it clear that he was very happy for her to stay. Then he left, shutting the door as quietly as he could behind him.

The morning was difficult. No, complicated. Trying to do his job, which, although not exactly intellectually demanding, did require care because Post Office procedures meant everything had to be correctly marked and noted and collated. But that wasn't the problem because he was diligent enough by nature, it was the way the ground seemed to have shifted underneath him. Why would it be such a big thing if he now had a lodger? True, she had arrived in slightly unusual circumstances; she was a girl and she was black - he could say the words, but he didn't really know what it might mean, though nothing at all at the moment, as far as he could tell; she had been hurt somehow - 'rape' was not a word which had real significance in his life experience; he had said he was happy for her to stay, but no need for anything to get pushed out because of that - though he would somehow have to modify the 'sofa' into something that would pass as a bed - the rest of last night must have been very uncomfortable to judge by all the aches he had when he woke up. But that was it, there was nothing really that anyone else would notice - except Frank of course when he next came round.

(Actually he was wrong because the chief clerk had thought several times during the morning that diligent Harry seemed rather distracted, though he was prepared to put it down to too much alcohol on a Friday evening, just this once.)

Yes, Frank. This was not the sort of thing that would ever happen to Frank! What would he say? He preferred to think of his mother and he remembered that she had once told him how she had taken in a ragged black girl running in the street outside their house carrying a little white kitten, because she was being chased by two angry men. He had a very dim memory of a little black girl - little, but bigger than he was - staying in their house with her kitten. His sisters played with her, though they were older, and his mother made a huge fuss over her. He thought his father was not very pleased, but maybe he was wrong about that. And then one day, she was gone. Nobody explained to him. He was only 4, but his mother had been sad for a long time.

When Harry arrived home just after midday, Nobomi was not there. His stomach turned. And then panic, his head started whirling and he rushed around the room turning things over, looking in corners, tearing off the bed covers, standing in the middle of the room his hands on his head in despair. He went out onto the corridor, looked along it both ways, down into the street, finally running into the road and peering helplessly into the distance in both directions. Eventually he hauled himself back up to his room and collapsed onto the bed. And fell asleep.

When he woke she was sitting by the bed.

"I had a little money. I went out to buy something for us to eat. When I came back you were here asleep. I just waited. Like you did."

It must be relief he was feeling. His whole body relaxed, he thought he could feel his muscles warmly tingling. Then his reserved English-young-man leapt in and he was scrambling to his feet, but she caught his arm and held it and looked straight into his eyes - was that the first time? - and said, "I want to tell you about me."

For the next two hours they sat together on the sofa.

Nobomi began:

"Do you know what the name of my home place means? It means "the ducks have flown away". Perhaps I am one of the ducks. Don't you think that's funny?

"I am Xhosa, but Matatiele is from the Sotho language. There are as many Xhosa as Sotho and we don't fight.

"It is so different from here. There is not really even a village. Most people live in houses on the plain and each house has its own space and each family has its cows. But everything is open. There are only a few fences.

"I think we must be quite high up, because it is much colder than here. And you can see very big mountains in the distance in a long line. We call them *intaba wenamba*. I think in English it is dragon mountain."

She paused. Then Harry:

"Matatiele means 'the ducks have flown'." She nodded. "And you might be like one of those ducks." She nodded again. "But what does *your* name mean?"

"Nobomi is a Xhosa word. It means life."

"I like that names can mean something. I think people can grow into their names. I think Harry means home ruler, but I prefer to look on it as home protector or defender... but I think I have a long way to go to grow into my name."

"Harry would be Mkhuseli in Xhosa."

He tried to say it and stumbled, but in the end... "That is quite close, Mkhuseli."

"Do you think your name has given you something?"

"I had not thought about that." She paused. "If life is spirit, then I think so. Spirit can go anywhere, it is free." She paused again. "But spirit is ancestors and ancestors means ancestral land and my family left their ancestral land, and now I have left my family."

For a moment she looked troubled. Then: "But I could not stay. It is very poor there. Our farm could not support all of us and I was the cleverest. I had to go."

"Was it difficult to say goodbye?"

"I did not say goodbye. I just walked away, before anyone got up. They would have made me stay. But I had to go. I think my father knew."

"I'm sorry. That is very lonely. Walking away on your own."

"I left a note. My sisters could read it to my parents. I knew which track I had to take. I just walked. I didn't turn round. I didn't look back."

Then: "Do you think I am bad?"

"You cannot be bad. You're nobomi."

Conversations often seem to have an inbuilt rhythm, they grow and they subside, and sometimes comes a natural lull, a pause, a taking of breath, like the rounding of the phrase line in a piece of music, and then they start again.

This was how it was that Saturday in a dingy room at 45 Fitzpatrick Road, East London on 14th July 1900.

Harry was not so used to talking about himself, he was the youngest of 3 brothers and 3 sisters and it had always seemed to him that no-one was ever interested in what he might say. It could have meant that he would turn in on himself and became introverted, but that was not how he had developed. He was naturally curious about things and was always looking to see what he could discover about any situation in which he found himself. And he liked exploring and finding new places, though always on his own. He would come home with stories about anything new he had found, and, though it seemed no-one was interested, because no-one seemed to have his curiosity about things, he still told them. And so it was that he had not lost his enquiring and curious mind, just because no-one seemed to listen, but had become quite carefree and able to be one of those people who do things because they are there to be done, and when that's finished, there will be something else.

In one of the silent moments, the rounding at the end of a phrase line, Nobomi asked, "Can we eat now?"

And so they ate. And the conversation started up again, because sharing a meal, like sharing talking, is so deep in our nature, and both nourish our spirit.

By the time the final lull came in their conversation they were sitting side by side at the head of the bed. Harry stood up as Nobomi sank down beneath the blanket - did they realise they were going separate ways? - and both said "goodnight" in the total darkness.

~~~

Letter from Hugh to Barbara 20th August 1948

Dear Barbara

Thank you for your letter. It seems to have been a bit delayed getting here. Philosophical was good. Like I said, thoughtful discussions about the nature and meaning of life are not what the Army goes in for. You don't think, you just _do_ (as you're told of course). But I don't mind exercising my brain for a change, though I'm probably a bit tram-lined compared to you. I remember my father confronting me with that quite often - "mind you don't get stuck in the tramlines" he told me when he was teaching me to drive, but he was really talking about life, not just driving. I think he might have been a bit like your brother Peter. I wouldn't mind meeting Peter.

I am going to let your 'Life' ideas float around in my mind and see where they go for me. First sense is a sort of relief. So if we accept deep down the play of life and death, do you think it can take away some of our anxiety? It would suggest we get anxious because we are avoiding _really_ seeing and accepting that there is an end, rather than just carrying on as if we are immortal?

conversations...1

I really think people's ideas are starting to loosen up and, I'm sure you're right, it's probably all to do with going through the War. I got a letter while I was at home this last time from a friend who had been taken prisoner and was held in a POW camp near Görlitz. He said that there was a French composer called Olivier someone, also a prisoner there, and he talked a lot about rhythm and time in music representing the intertwining of life and death and how he was already planning a symphony for after the War using these ideas. (Sounds like it would be a rather long symphony.) My friend said this chap got together the three other professional musicians in the camp and wrote a quartet for them, which they played to the residents and camp guards. Apparently he called it 'Quartet for the End of Time'. I can't imagine how that went down in a POW camp!

Life and death carries on here in the same way. The devastation is horrific, but even worse is what it means. The housing problem is much much worse than the UK which could be because there isn't the equivalent of all the prefab estates there are in the UK and there isn't even the money because of what the Austrians have to pay - to keep <u>us,</u> apart from anything else. I am in the city now. I don't like it. You're hedged around with rules and protocols. Everybody is obsessed about what the 'other lot' are doing - even between allies. There's no trust and it's common knowledge there are a lot of spies and informants everywhere. You never know what's safe. The place has quite a sinister feel about it most of the time.

What about you? Has your claustrophobic feeling kept at bay and is your goodwill towards your household things still in place? I hope so.

I appreciate you writing to me very much,

Hugh

the fourth room

On Monday 25th June 1902 Richard-Symons boarded the SS Saxon of the Union-Castle Line in Southampton. It was an almost new mail ship, the pride of the Line apparently, fast and reliable, and had been used frequently as a troop carrier during the Boer War. There were some troops, he noticed, on this voyage, but, after the peace treaty, there were more coming back than going out. In any case the troops travelled third class and were kept well away from the upper decks where the first class cabins were located.

His journey down to Southampton by train had been tedious. He was a printer and publisher, a business in which there are always deadlines to meet and a constant throng of impatient clients to satisfy, and so the necessity to take 3 months away from the business to make this trip (he had no idea yet that it would in fact be much longer) was inconvenient and costly. He had staff of course and he had had to delegate his most trusted employee to take urgent decisions in his absence (because he felt he could not put all his trust in the telegraph service from so far away); but there was still material to read assess and edit in order to keep the business prospering. And so it was that the crush and disturbance in his train compartment (despite travelling first class) had been a considerable annoyance and it was a great relief when he was finally aboard the Saxon, though even then all the waving and tears and general hullabaloo of send-offs going on around him was too much and he demanded of the steward that he be taken by the speediest route possible to his cabin. Once there he took out the ship's 'Notes for First Class Passengers' and planned how he would organise his days for the next 3 weeks on board (the Saxon would only take two weeks to arrive at Cape Town but East London was the second call after that). Then he called the steward back to unpack and arrange his clothes and settled into a leisurely freshening toiletry session before dinner.

He lowered himself into his bath and after a few minutes went into one of those in-between states where you are conscious of where you are, but thoughts become ephemeral and transient, with impossibly fast scene changes and disturbing shifts from one muddled view to another. Harry appeared, but many years younger, and then Fanny his wife, and there was Frank trying to explain something to him but he didn't want to listen, and he was watching Harry again swimming at the Lido - he was a good strong swimmer... He was a good strong swimmer. How could he have drowned?

He was alone and he drowned. What was it like when he knew he was going to lose? Did it hurt not to be able to say goodbye to his father? And then Fanny was back: "... of all of our children, Richard, it's Harry that can hold on when he wants and let go when he wants and he seems equally content with whatever comes up and just sails through"... Just sails through. But not this time.

Richard-Symons hauled himself from his bath, dried himself off and applied his preferred cologne. He dressed for dinner, and then wondered whether he shouldn't order his dinner in his cabin - the first night of a voyage and people will be sure to be asking questions. That will present him with the awkward issue of what and how much to say; would he talk about his business? (he wouldn't dare mention family), could he use poor health as a topic? (but a voyage to South Africa at the end of a nasty war was not a very likely health cure), could he turn the tables and be the one who was always asking the questions? (but he was not sure he had the strength for that, not tonight), or could he keep his distance, be in his own world, and vague when he did have to contribute to conversation? Maybe that was the best policy. He left his cabin and made his way to the first class dining saloon in the middle of the ship. Dinner only though, he would not sit around talking in the lounge afterwards, he must see that he finished his drinks with the meal.

To his dismay when he arrived in the dining saloon he was seated at the only table remaining which had a spare place, and at which sat a single lady. His unease had increased as he came closer and saw that she was younger than he thought it fitting for him to join alone for dinner. He had motioned to the steward to see whether there was another place, but to no avail as all the other diners at this sitting appeared to have started and indeed this lady herself was already consuming her soup. As he was being seated by the steward he apologised for being tardy and causing this interruption to her meal whereupon she looked up unperturbed and said, "You are not inconveniencing me at all, Sir."

Richard-Symons was relieved to be presented with the menu very quickly, the serving of the sitting already being underway, and so he was able to absorb himself with studying this and then the wine list and thus delay the awkwardness of introductions. But in reality it amounted to less than two minutes before he had to make some gesture:

"May I introduce myself, Miss, my name is Richard-Symons, though Richard is how I prefer to be addressed."

"It is a pleasure Mr Richard… "

"No just Richard, I assure you." He thought: I suppose it is just possible she may make a connection if I give her my family name (and in fact it is possible that she could have done, though in all the time they were to spend together she never did.)

"My name is Isabella Davy. Just Isabella, please." She considered his formal dress and its quality and went on, "I am afraid, Richard, that to sit with me, could be a little below your usual position. In fact I feel an imposter here, because I am only paid for second class and should not be in this saloon at all. The fact is the captain is a friend of a friend of my father and upgraded my booking and the first I knew of it was when I got on board. And so here I am, feeling very out place."

Richard-Symons fumbled for a response: "I assure you, you do not look or act at all out of place."

"Thank you, Sir."

"Now, I see your place has not been laid with a wine glass - may I invite you to join me in a glass with your meal?"

"I drink very little alcohol, but I think a small glass of dry white wine would suit me very well"

"It is done."

Richard-Symons rarely drank white wine (always preferring a claret) but he indicated an appropriate bottle when the waiter came to take his order. Then, seeing that the lady had already almost finished her soup, he of course declined the first course out of courtesy.

In his playing out in his head of some of the uncomfortable possibilities for the evening that he had engaged in before he left his cabin, this one had not occurred to him. Certainly the tactic which he had lighted on as the safest, to keep his distance and stay sheltered in his own world, would be socially inappropriate, if not rude, in the company of a lady on her own.

He would have to start somewhere: "You say that you feel out of place, but so, in a different way, do I. It is in fact quite unusual for me to dine out other than as a business function and apart from that I eat always with my family." He went on quickly, "To be in the exclusive company of a lady, young lady, and unexpectedly sharing dinner is, well, to be honest, completely unknown for me. So if I do or say anything which in the least discomforts you, please tell me clearly and I will desist."

She gave him a smile which was soft, but not in any seductive way, and understanding, yes, that was it, understanding, as if she saw, somehow, below the surface.

"I am completely at my ease, Mr Richard, sorry, Richard."

When they were settled into eating their first courses, he asked: "I am interested in how a lady comes to be travelling on her own to South Africa at such a time as this. Of course the war is over, but only just, and I am imagining that large parts of the country are still coping with the repercussions and might be quite unsettled."

"The war is why I am here. I am sent by the War Victims Relief Committee set up by the Society of Friends. I am a nurse and the Society of Friends has long been campaigning for better conditions and more nurses in the camps. I have always felt a Quaker in my roots - both my parents were Quaker Members - and I was sent to a Quaker school and have always attended Meetings when I could, so, being a nurse as well, I thought I could offer myself. And my cousin is taking up a new position in Pretoria next year."

"I stand in admiration of such a commitment. But even so, a young lady on her own."

"There are others there when I arrive."

"It is the camps which concern you?"

"The conditions are inhuman."

"I believe you, but war is war."

"War is war and Quakers are pacifists, Richard. The taking of human life on any pretext cannot be justified." And then because it was not in her nature to cause another's discomfort: "But what about you, Richard, this is taking you a long way from your home too. Do you have children?"

"Yes, I have si…" His voice trailed off. A lump came to his throat. He closed his eyes to hold in the tears and quickly raised his napkin to his face with the pretence of wiping his lips but also held it to his eyes, "I have five", replaced his napkin and quickly resumed eating.

Isabella was troubled. She had tried not to confront what might be Richard's prejudice in order to avoid discord, but had opened a wound instead.

"Please forgive me." But he was already far away from the first class dining saloon of the SS Saxon.

They were almost at the end of the main course before their silence was broken.

Richard-Symons thought it was his place to recover what he could: "You must think me very rude to have broken off without explanation like that..."

"Not at all, and please don't think you have to say any more, but your company gives me great pleasure and I only hope my accidental insensitivity won't mean..."

"The fact is I had six children, three boys and three girls, but now... this is...," Richard-Symons took a slow deep breath, "it is why I am here, because the youngest drowned some weeks ago in the ocean off East London." He rushed the words out but felt relief, though it seemed his whole body was shaking. He hardly heard his companion when she said, "East London is where I am going too", but if he had heard he might have noticed her tone as slightly puzzled.

A waiter was hovering to clear the plates and dishes and another to take an order for their desserts, but he intervened and said, "No, we will have coffee now, in the lounge."

Richard-Symons got up and made to help his companion from the table, but she was already following, not with any pique that this man had offered her no choice, but with relief for him that he had recovered control, even though at another time he would see himself as having achieved this only by grossly transgressing the norms of etiquette.

To sit in the lounge was a relief for both. Tension is often resolved with a change of scene and sometimes even the same subject matter when started afresh can seem less charged with emotion. This was the case tonight.

Isabella said: "Richard, I am very sorry that this voyage is one of sadness for you. When you indicated the circumstances, I found myself saying without really thinking that I was also going to East London, instead of expressing my sorrow for you. But since that is the case we have the time, if you wanted, that is, you will want to prepare yourself and if I could help in any way and that was your wish, I will be here to the end of your voyage."

"Thank you, Miss Isabella. I think it will be my wish, but for the moment, I feel I have travelled a very long way in a very short time and I must allow myself some recovery. I wish to retire, but I would not leave you alone…"

"I feel likewise. Would you be able to walk me to my cabin on your way?"

"Of course."

And so the first day of Richard-Symons' voyage into a darkness which he could never have contemplated, drew to its close.

~~~

On 10th January 1901, some 18 months before this voyage, the Cape Town correspondent of the Nelson Daily Miner filed this report to his newspaper:

AT HEAVY COST

Cycling Corps Capture a Pass with Heavy Casualties.

Cape Town, Jan, 10,— The cyclist corps, which left here Saturday, occupied Pickaneer's Kloof Sunday after a race with the Boers for its possession. The Republicans attempted to intercept the cyclists but the latter succeeded in occupying the position, though three of them were killed and twenty-three wounded. The cyclists retain the pass. The commandeering of horses has commenced in the districts where owners have refused to sell them to the military authorities.

The casualties to which the report referred were later established as 4 killed and 23 wounded. Later still it was reported that of the 23 wounded (some severely), 16 had been hit by rifle fire, 3 by Maxim machine-gun fire (the weapon having previously been taken by a Boer unit from a British position elsewhere that had been wiped out) and 4 had been injured when a section of the path they were taking to establish a strongpoint overlooking the Boer emplacement gave way and resulted in their falling between 20 and 50 feet down a rock outcrop. There being no regimental aid post with the cycle corps and transport from the location in the dark being too hazardous, temporary field dressings were improvised and the wounded were finally taken late the next day to the general hospital at Piketberg for onward transport where necessary.

~~~

Richard-Symons fell asleep quickly, though he awoke two hours later as the ship started to roll. This was the first time that it had really occurred to him that he was at sea, and the inevitable associations which that brought were at once troubling. The half-formed fading images of his bath-time were back, only this time sudden flashes inserted themselves into the passing scenes, flashes which were not so much bursts of light as other images completely filling his vision for an instant without warning and then disappearing before he could discern what they were. He decided he should not risk sitting up or getting out of bed, given the rolling of the ship and his parlous mental control, and so he lay. After a while he noticed that, though lying out in the bed, he had his arms around his chest as if he were hugging himself and that this seemed to give him some relief. Then he wondered if he could find other physical comfort and turned on his side, drawing his legs towards his chest. This too seemed to help. He had no idea now of the time passing, only that whatever had been happening with the images in his head was becoming less alarming. And he thought he also heard his dinner companion saying, "...East London is where I am going, I will be here to the end..." - no that's not right... to the end of what? I'm going to East London to find Harry. And with that he fell asleep once more.

Isabella was used to facing the plethora of feelings which came up for her in her work and could seem to be contradictory in paradoxical ways; it had happened often during the last year or so while she had been working in the camps in South Africa. So to simply feel a little dazed from her evening's experience was not in itself difficult for her. But this was more disorientated than dazed. Not by the person or the company of Richard-Symons though, more a sense of something not quite revealed; she remembered St Paul, "For now we see through a glass darkly" and she felt a shiver run through her body. Would she have been helped in this moment by a version, which appeared some years after her death: "At present we see only puzzling reflections in a mirror, but one day we shall see face to face"? But for Isabella in this moment no easy unravelling. She knew that she was not a good sleeper on these voyages and so she patiently sat and read, hoping that soon she would feel the need to lie down. And as the ship began to roll, she too saw a young man struggling against unequal odds, and to her too came the question, "What is it like when you know you are going to lose?"

The next day was calm and bright as the ship, set now on a course due south, crossed the Bay of Biscay and started to feel the swell of the Atlantic Ocean as it lost sight of the Spanish coast.

Richard-Symons, concerned not to let himself slip into a blissful indolence as the weather improved with their southward course, nor sink into maudlin inactivity, had created a schedule for himself which meant that he would rise at 7, perform his toilet, have a coffee (which he instructed the steward to bring at 7.45) and then work through to midday. At midday he would lie down for half an hour (earlier than he would have done at home, but it appeared that the ship's time for serving its luncheon was one o'clock). He would eat in his cabin and then read a book (simply for the pleasure of reading) for about an hour before emerging into the upper saloon or the deck bar simply to stroll around the various deck spaces and lounges. If he happened to meet Isabella on his perambulation that would be good and they would doubtless exchange words, but he felt no urgency to be immersed again in conversation as he was the previous evening. He had no doubt that it would happen and he felt only a passing disquiet at the prospect, the more so because, in a way, they had pre-arranged that it should.

That day, a Tuesday, he emerged onto the upper deck at 3 and did in fact meet Isabella as she was sitting reading. They greeted each other and exchanged the normal pleasantries before arranging to meet before dinner in the first class lounge for a pre-prandial (though he hastily added that he quite accepted that she might decline any alcohol before the meal) and then they parted. Richard-Symons was pleased to observe that he could still maintain an air of equanimity against the backdrop of personal tragedy.

Over their pre-dinner drinks, he tested out how secure was his self-control, in the way that he knew best, by inviting the other person to comment first on a subject that was sensitive for him. So to Isabella: "I am in awe of someone such as yourself, Isabella, who puts themselves in the way of distressing, if not dangerous, situations, when there is no necessity driving such action. It feels as if I have hidden behind the belief that this war was a necessity, because keeping the British Empire intact is all-important, for the native peoples as well, it being a way of educating them and making their lives better."

"That is what the British people are told," responded Isabella, "the newspaper owners put out this message and the people feel patriotic and then they get more excited and start to believe there is only one right message, especially with all the leaflets and pamphlets that appear. I would like to be able to take on the publishers of all that sort of disreputable material."

"I don't imagine publishers believe all the words they print for their clients."

"Then they are being dishonest by publishing, do you not think?" (Richard-Symons was relieved when she went straight on.) "But there *is* necessity for me to do this. I am a Quaker, so I am a pacifist. Some in our Society campaigned politically against the War, but we could not win that campaign against powerful people and the government, and even the Queen, so we have to help the victims in any way we can. And when Kitchener decided to drive everyone off the land, the Boers *and* the natives, and put them in these camps... do you know more people die in these camps than live? Most people die from disease, especially cholera. And mainly it is the children and the old people who die. And the government does nothing - no clean water, little food, only a few nurses, no medicines." After a pause, "It is a necessity for me to do what I do."

At this point the steward came to show them into dinner. After the gap in their conversation while the first courses were ordered, Isabella might have changed the topic, but, ever the campaigner at heart, she pressed one last point: "Perhaps, if my argument is new to you Richard, you might be in a position to spread the message yourself. I don't mean become a Quaker - though I am sure you would be received - but maybe you have other means. If time allowed, and were it not for the tragedy which has brought you on this voyage, I would have liked to give you some first-hand acquaintance with what is happening here."

Isabella knew that her last remark (or was it her single-minded insistence on bringing in her own issues?) had made him uncomfortable. He had shifted in his seat, looked down at his plate, and now he was silent.

What had she done? She truly appreciated being able to be there with him. She felt off-balance. "I'm being insensitive. I'm sorry."

"Not at all, you are... you are..."

"I can't imagine what it was like to find out from so far away, from a stranger, how could you..."

"No not a stranger, it was another son who sent a telegram and then I was able to phone. He was in a hotel in East London, I don't know why. There has been nothing since. He was buried the day after he was found, Frank said. But I want him to have a proper grave and headstone. The youngest. I couldn't just leave him. I have to know where he is." He realised he must have been almost incoherent, rambling in a way not at all like the man he usually was.

"So Frank was with him."

"Not swimming with him. Just in East London in this hotel. But why? Frank was supposed to be... somewhere else, in Western Cape I think. It was Frank that got Harry to come out here. And then he left him and went somewhere else." After a long pause: "That was the first time we had heard from Frank for almost a year."

"Harry had his brother close by again though, in those last days."

"Yes, there is that." After another pause: "There is a lot I have to learn."

Isabella wondered whether this last remark had more than a surface meaning.

In due time the end of the main course offered a relief of the tension, though on this occasion they decided to take the dessert, after which they both agreed that they would prefer to have coffee in their cabins and so they retired.

~~~

From 1899 to 1902 a British Boer War surgeon, Major Frederick Porter, writing home to his wife, often noted that many times more soldiers were dying from sepsis and infected wounds and disease than were killed by direct enemy action. Insanitary conditions and lack of clean water were in fact the biggest killers. In January 1901 he wrote:

> *Another, and a very important cause of the infection of wounds was on many occasions the impossibility of obtaining at the front water of a quality suitable for the preparation of antiseptic solutions, without an ample supply of which aseptic or antiseptic surgery is, of course, out of the question. The water on which the field hospitals and bearer companies' dressing stations had to depend for this purpose was often muddy and incapable of filtration through a Berkfeld filter, and, it could not be boiled for want of fuel. Naturally, under these circumstances, wounds became infected during the necessary dressings….*

~~~

<u>Letter from Frank to Fanny on 20th May 1902</u>

My dear mother,

I have tried to imagine the anguish and distress that my news about Harry has caused you all, but especially you, dear Mama. Of course I cannot come close to feeling your agony and in a way it is a relief to me that I cannot, but I would so much like to be able to say something to you which might relieve your pain. Alas I do not know how. I can only tell you that Harry and I were doing well together since I arrived back from Western Cape and that Harry was not troubled during this time… he had that regular job with the Post Office here that I set up for him to come out to, and he had a girl-friend and that made him happy too because they were serious about each other. She is a native girl called Nobomi and she had walked here from the furthest corner of Eastern Cape. (That is a very long way.) We were actually wondering how he could bring her back to England. She is from a people who were known as Wanderers. So I would like you to try not to fret that Harry's life was bad in some way or difficult to bear. You know that Harry and I are very different characters. Having said that, we had been getting on together better here than we had ever got on, though that did not mean that we spent all our time together. We very rarely went down to the beach together, because Harry just went to swim, and you know I had never been able to swim like he could. I was not there that evening and I have spent many hours in self-recrimination that I could not have been able to be at his side, though I do not believe that I could have saved him. For that I ask your forgiveness.

I know that Father is already on his way here and I will be sure to be on the quay when his ship arrives. It will be difficult for him, all that way on his own, without your loving company. But I feel for you in your loneliness while he is gone, always thinking about the day he will return to you. I know you are not alone: you have four of us there to help you, and if I can count as well from so far away, I am there too, in spirit of course.

Are you wondering about me? I know that I have not been in touch for a long time, because my life seems never to have been still enough to write. I think I told you that I was going down to Cape Town after I had settled Harry in. That was to help out in the small way I could with, well, I suppose you would call it the 'war effort'. Not to be a soldier, but to join the first of the Cape Cycle Corps. These are small units on bicycles - yes, bicycles - who now keep most of the communications going between the units that are actually doing the fighting, taking instructions out from the field command posts to the lines, carrying despatches, taking orders back to base for supplies, that sort of thing. They started because the Boers were coming over into Cape Province and the British Army had to organise efficiently and economically to prevent them hurting our people. Anyway I am back now in East London and the only sign of the war here is all the troops getting onto ships to go home. Of course doing something so very different affects one, but I suppose that happens with any change of scene in life. We are always changed too. But more of that another time. This letter was really to be about you and I just put that in because I thought you would want to know. I have felt a little guilty for not writing for so long. In my defence I can only say that it has been very difficult. But I promise that I will tell you more as I recover here. At the moment I am living in Harry's lodgings at 45 Fitzpatrick Road, East London, Eastern Cape and I will telegraph you if that changes.

So to you, dear Mama, and also to Nora, Jenifer, Louie and Barry I send my love and sincere condolences in this horrible time for us all.

Your loving son,
Frank

On the day before the SS Saxon arrived in East London, towards the end of June, Frank received a letter from his youngest sister Louie (5 years his junior):

Dear Frank

Mother has asked me to write and thank you for your letter. She couldn't face writing now but she will I know, very soon. It was a great relief to us all to hear from you. We have been thinking of you all the time and just hoping you would break your silence soon. Of course we did not know the reason for your silence, and you have still not really told us, but at least we know you are still alive. At this time it seems so important that we are all able to feel together, even though we are spread over such a great distance. I worked out from an atlas that you are about 10,000 miles away from us! I have no idea what that means really.

We try our best to imagine what things are like for you, but I do not think we come very close. We have seen that the War is over and that must be good. But if we are honest we have not taken in much about it, although we see the newspapers and the leaflets and things that Father's company prints and they have all seemed very supportive of the cause and how our boys are doing. But I suppose it looks very different if it is all around you. I know that mother would be much happier if you were not in Africa. I believe she is scared all the time, Frank, and now Father is on his way too... she just wants you both home. Can't you come home now?

That's a silly question. Is this female intuition? I don't know, but I do think there is something you haven't told us. I hope you will tell us everything in your next letter and I hope that will come soon. I always liked the way you and I seemed to have a special connection. I suppose that happens in large families. But what are you not telling me Frank?

So here's the last thing.

You will have found the locket in the envelope. Mother said I had to send it and I did not follow the whole story, but I will do my best. Here goes. The locket was given to her by her father when her mother, who was also called Fanny, died. The picture inside is a photograph of her mother, which her father had put in for her. He said he had cut it out of a studio photograph of the whole family, cat as well, which her mother is holding, as you see. (Before you ask, I don't know its name, maybe it was 'Whitey'.) Don't go away, that's not the end. Her father was precise about who had to have the locket after her. Apparently he believed in life-gifts not death-gifts, so passing things on during your lifetime, and he also wanted to respect his Fanny's belief that the women and the youngest boys should come in for some things by right. When mother read about Harry having a girl friend (his first as far as we know, and now of course his only) and with Harry being the youngest and her favourite - sorry, Frank - somehow she decided that the locket had to go to the last woman who knew him. Her logic did not completely convince me, but anyway, that is what she wants. So here it is. Please will you give it to Nobomi?

Right, that's it. My wrist is tired. I cannot write any more. Now you owe me, and remember - no omissions and no fibs.

Love to you brother,
Louie

ps. can you send us a photograph of Nobomi?

~~~

Isabella was in her early thirties and after school had trained as a nurse and had worked in that capacity in her native Yorkshire ever since. She had not married, though she had come close. It would seem a slightly frivolous analogy, but nevertheless quite apt, to liken her unmarried state to that of a nun, though in her case "married to Christ" would be supplanted by "married to those who suffer", and would not presuppose celibacy. The religious connotation, though, is appropriate, because, though never becoming a Member of a particular Meeting (because she moved around so much), Isabella attended at whichever meeting of the Friends was closest to her. Her parents, themselves Members, had sent her to a Quaker boarding school just before she was 10 and she discovered that she valued the special kind of intimacy she found in the silences of Friends' meetings.

Many women of her time who chose nursing as their mission in life grew to portray their calling with a likeness which displayed the earnestness that their practice demanded of them. Isabella was different. She was slight (beneath the modestly voluminous nurse's uniform of the time) and her face seemed naturally formed in a soft smile, as if completely incapable of any tension which might imply criticism or even disquiet. Men of all ages (and many women) found themselves drawn to her, with her aura of intuitive sensibility and gentle openness.

For Richard-Symons, in his emotional plight, her presence was like manna from heaven, but even though he quickly felt relief from having her as dinner companion, he could not have envisaged the extent of her influence on his life over the coming months, and the traces it would leave.

On the fourth evening over the dessert Isabella noticed that her companion appeared more solemn than previously. They had talked little over the main course and what they had exchanged seemed quite light and harmless, mostly her schooling in her Quaker boarding school. Richard-Symons had asked again about the Friends' principles and it might have sounded like a way to oil the cogs of polite dinner conversation, but Isabella knew that it was not that and that something had come into his mind which cast a shadow - of regret? she wondered - that would not simply dissolve. But when he spoke, it was not to go immediately back to Harry. "It is strange," he said "how, when we are growing up, we think that everyone's experience is like our own, and stranger still that we go on thinking it."

"I thought my school-time was how it was for everyone, but yours was very different, and not just because it was a boarding school, whereas mine was a day-school. Mine was all about achievement and getting on, but yours seems to have been more about how to be a good person and part of the family of those around you. Mine was about competition and yours seems to have been about cooperation."

"It was not always as altruistic as you make it sound. We had some bad eggs, who couldn't simply keep quiet and let others get what they could out of the deep moments. Just because they couldn't do it themselves. But it is so often the case, is it not, that people decry and even make fun of what they do not understand?" Then, "But I am sure you are right, there was a difference of emphasis, of philosophy I suppose, aside from the difference because of mine being Quaker: yours was preparing people to make more and have more, and mine seemed to just want people to develop and have a friendly attitude."

Now Richard-Symons thought about Harry, or, to be precise, he thought about how *he* was different with Harry and Frank. He felt he could see where Frank was going and he could be comfortable talking to him because they seemed be on a similar tack, even though he could not understand why Frank wanted to throw away the family business and come out here to South Africa, yes, that was a stupid mistake but perhaps he will see sense. But Harry, with Harry he felt quite torn. He had to admit that he had always found him an odd boy with all the unusual things he noticed and the way he always seemed so self-sufficient and happy to be on his own; but for him, as his father, and Harry being the youngest, he had yearned to be close to him, and when Harry wanted to follow Frank, he had felt it such a wrench.

"He didn't know what he was doing to me," he said out loud, without realising it.

"That must be so hard, when you have to let a child follow their own path." Isabella surprised herself with her response, because she realised that she had not really known where Richard-Symons was in his thoughts.

"Harder now, when you are forced to re-examine your own principles for life: it is a father's job to pass on their knowledge of what is right to their children, especially their sons."

"As Quakers we see that with a different emphasis, that it is our responsibility to allow everybody, which of course means our children as well, the silence to find and express who they are and to respect them for that. Maybe the difference in our schooling is connected with that as well."

"Do you, or perhaps I should say, would you, have children, Isabella?"

"Alas no. I would like to. I have known romance, but I had to make a choice. My beliefs and my calling in nursing did not offer the likelihood of a home life which could be possible for the man I loved." His face must have shown surprise. "Ah, don't misunderstand me, Richard, I am not claiming anything as exalted as a nun's devotion. But I needed to be the person I am. Perhaps if I had met a doctor." A hint of an impertinent smile flashed across her face.

"My Fanny would have been a musician. She gave that up to have our family. I have only just begun to understand what that meant. Meant for her and meant about me. So I admire you... but I am also thankful Fanny was not like you." This time it was his turn for an impertinent smile.

Through their successive evenings, Richard-Symons found himself increasingly drawn to the quiet and unwavering sincerity of his companion and the simple way in which she expressed her own beliefs and ideas without ever implying a misjudgment in others for their beliefs. Once they had even talked about her mission to South Africa during the Boer War to minister in the concentration camps to the Boers, though little (and this perplexed him) to the natives, many of whom were in similar and adjacent camps with far inferior conditions. To his surprise he had found himself expressing with some indignation his distaste that such care was given to the group who were in fact the enemy and not to the innocent onlookers, the native Africans.

"But all are equal," Isabella had replied. It occurred to Richard-Symons that this argument cut both ways, but he held his tongue.

As their conversations tracked the ship's steady course down the west coast of the vast African continent, Richard-Symons became increasingly aware of how much their exchanges had become a feature of his life which he would miss when they came to an end.

"You said that you were staying on the ship as far as East London, did you not?" he asked as they approached Cape Town, with the Cape of Good Hope in the distance.

"That's right, and then I take the train to Kronstaadt, which someone told me is about 500 miles. There is a camp there. But there is also a new camp in East London itself and it was mentioned to me that the Friends had no-one available to help there and they might want me to take that position for a while. It all seems a little uncertain, but I have to remain in East London for a few days anyway to obtain a permit to travel to Kronstaadt."

"You have somewhere to stay."

"Oh yes, I will be staying with a minister in East London."

"Well, I believe that I shall be living at the Beach Hotel on the Esplanade, and I would be most honoured if you saw fit to keep in touch, perhaps you would join me, no us, that is Frank as well as myself, for a meal one day."

"Thank you Richard, that is a very kind offer and I hope that we will be able to share some more time, on dry land finally."

arrivals

On Sunday 15th December 1901 Harry and Nobomi were waiting on the platform of East London station for the arrival of Frank's train from Kimberley. Train times were only approximate if they were given out at all. The impetus for the building of the railways had been commercial, primarily the transport of gold and diamonds to the coastal ports for shipment. Freight trains might carry some passengers and there were a few passenger-only services, but all non-commercial traffic was subordinated to the commercial, and everything took second place to military requirements.

They had been waiting since 10 in the morning, the earliest time there could be an arrival from Kimberley, even if the train had stopped overnight 'just' up the line at Queenstown, though that was itself over 100 miles distant. So they had brought food and they waited, which was easier for Nobomi than for Harry. To simply allow the next thing to happen when it will, is in the nature of someone who has grown up in the vast spaces of the African continent and has been moulded by a culture which does not need the exigencies of starting times and closing times, where for centuries the rhythm of a life matched itself to the rhythms of its setting, its seasons, and the natural pattern of daylight and darkness. In contrast, Harry's upbringing and culture bred anxiety and impatience, though he himself, in comparison with his peers, was a model of carefree spontaneity.

The platform filled up during the morning because it was known that this train would be bringing passengers, but it was not until the middle of the afternoon that word started to circulate amongst those waiting that it was not far up the line now. By this time there was also a small army corps at the far end of the platform - it was presumed, because there were going to be Boer commandos being taken into detention.

As the activity increased, so did Harry's restlessness. From sitting on a bench, the two of them holding hands, he now took to getting up and pacing the platform, returning to the bench and reporting that nothing was in sight yet. Nobomi saw his tension and felt his nervousness and wished that the calm she could create for herself by being completely still in her body and her mind, she could wrap in a pouch for him to hold near his heart.

Frank had done his best to prepare them with the essentials of his story, the action at Pickaneer's Kloof, a fall of fifty feet and rolling a hundred yards down a steep rocky face, his smashed leg trapped under a boulder, lying till daylight for release, the agony of evacuation, no field hospital, waiting a day for transport to Piketberg, his leg infected, the surgeon saying gangrene and his only hope a further amputation, will try to save your thigh but quickly now, transferred to Kimberley by ambulance and train, but still months in hospital fighting, fighting, fighting the infection the disbelief the melancholia, and now… not restored, but alive to start over.

The train ground slowly, noisily, into the station. The end of the line.

In Harry's mind - how was his brother even going to get down from the train? He was close now to the carriages, Nobomi clinging to his shirt, in the swirl of bodies and clutter of baggage and clambering, a babel of voices and jolting and waving and reaching and crying and… wounded bodies clumsily climbing down… and Frank, yes, Frank at the top of the steps waiting his turn… smiling - smiling? - of course smiling - it was over now - family again. Harry reached up and Frank, his one foot on the top step, had to lean out and trust that he would land upright and in the arms of his two protectors.

~~~

Letter from Frank to Louie 30th August 1902

Dear Louie

Thank you for your letter, which was like a wonderful bright light shining through the darkness of all the tragedy of the past months. I am hoping that you will be able to read my reply in private and then decide how you pass it on to the others. This is not because I want to be secretive and hide things, but because what I am going to say will be difficult for people to hear and comprehend, so it might be better if it were given to them gradually, or at least by someone who knows all and passes it on from their heart too. There now, already I have got you worried, but the worst you already know, about Harry. The rest is painful in parts, but nothing is as bad as losing Harry, remember that.

I am going to just tell you the things that happened in order first, just as you might read them in a newspaper. It will sound very impersonal, but it is probably easier that way, and then I will start over and talk about what it has all meant to me… and Father and how he is, because he is now here… and Nobomi, because I have given her the locket and I will tell you about that too.

It all started around the time of Harry's arrival here. I had set up up a job for him like I said I would, so that he had something to come to. It was a clerk job in the Post Office, but it was something steady and safe and offered prospects as the colony's economy developed. (The post and telegraph service is very important.) That all went well for him and he had already progressed a little in his responsibilities.

For me, things had come to a standstill by the time Harry arrived the October before last. I was in a drawing office doing calculations for new winching engines, but the government took over the work and moved it up to Kimberley because it was to do with the new mines and for a while I just did short jobs when somebody needed more hands.

One of the men I had been working with in the drawing office had gone down to Cape Town after the office closed and he sent me a letter saying that prospects down in that city were much better (it is bigger than East London) and in particular there were companies making bicycles for the Army, because Kitchener was reorganising after the disasters of 1899. There were going to be cycle corps in the army, sometimes attached to units and sometimes sent out from a base, not for fighting, but to do all the communications, carrying despatches, messages, that sort of thing, and bicycles were what he wanted because they made less noise than horses! Do you remember the bicycle I had at home which I modified to go faster by changing the pedals and the drive cogs? So it seemed just right for me and after I had made sure that Harry was settled in and happy I moved to Cape Town during November. The work was exactly what I could do and I made a lot of improvements for the company I worked for.

At the same time the war was changing and becoming dangerous for the people even as far down as Western Cape. The Boers were operating in 'commando' units and making strikes to destroy our farms in the country and capturing and often murdering our families. It did not happen like that in Cape Town itself, but these were still our people and had a right to settle and farm like anybody else. So I decided to join one of the Cycle Corps, because it meant I was making patriotic use of what I could do well, ride a bicycle. It wasn't really being a soldier, even though we had rifles which we could sling over our backs or even strap to the crossbar when we were riding - those were supposed to be just a precaution, because our real job was communications. But barely a month after I had joined word came through that a Boer commando unit was heading for an important mountain pass. I was in the nearest Cycle Corps and around 30 of us were sent from Cape Town to guard the pass and be on high ground before the Boers could get there. It was about 100 miles, but we arrived as it was getting dark and before the Boers. During the night we were changing position to surround the enemy and the path collapsed just in front of me and I fell in a landslide about 100 yards down the hillside. My leg became trapped between two large boulders. Several of the corps were killed by the

Boers and others were injured and I could not move. I had to wait till morning to be freed and then the whole day until they could take me to the nearest hospital. The pain got worse and worse during the day and I believe I was not really conscious when I arrived at the hospital, then I don't remember anything until I woke up about 5 days later. That was when they told me that the surgeon had amputated my lower right leg. They said that the field dressings had become infected and gangrene had started. It was the only way to stop the gangrene spreading and killing me. Eventually they moved me to a hospital in Kimberley because they could not get the operation to heal. They did another operation and took my knee. In the end my leg did heal, what was left of it, and they let me come back to East London because Harry was here. I arrived back in the middle of December. Harry and Nobomi met me. Harry had arranged a room for me on the ground floor at the Beach Hotel, which was a very good place to recuperate and it was quite close to his lodgings. He came and spent most evenings with me and Nobomi came every morning. I was very lucky.

I've rushed through that to get to the end. I don't like seeing the pictures that come up in my mind. I don't like thinking how completely without control I was. I don't like the feeling that it was not my body any longer, because even after they told me, I was sure my leg was still there, I could feel it. But it wasn't of course, that was my mind doing that, and then I thought my mind was going wrong.

I am very sorry, Louie, that I am telling you this. I felt I owed it to you, because you said "no omissions and no fibs". There is not really much more. You will guess that the pain at times was so awful, especially any time they transported me somewhere. And the melancholia, that got very black, but in the end, I have come back to what I knew, almost. Having some family to 'come home to' was wonderful - I *was smiling when I got off the train! Although I nearly fell off. And Nobomi felt like family too. No, she <u>feels</u> like family too. And here is your next shock. She is pregnant. You will be an aunt in about 7 months time. And Mama will be a grandmother. But of course still no Harry and we have not talked about what is going to happen. I am sure Father will have something to say about it. At the moment poor Father is in a daze. He had found some company on the passage down, a Quaker lady who was coming to help run one of the concentration camps they have here for people Kitchener drove out of their farms on the veldt. I think she might be a useful friend to have when Nobomi gets near the birth.*

We are all a bit lost, Sis. The world we knew seems to have left us. It is like we have to start again, but none of what we thought we knew about helps us. But try not to worry and tell Mama not to worry. We will find a way through and we will be back to you, but it is going to take longer than we would want or you expected.

I gave the locket to Nobomi and told her about it. She cried and said she would hold it always when she needed help. And the photo. That was a good idea you had, so yours is with the letter. But Nobomi had never seen a picture of herself, so I had the photographer do another for her and she said she would keep it always. She was very happy then.

That is all I can write now. I am truly exhausted, but I am also relieved because to tell you everything was always going to be the most difficult thing I could imagine. I know you already feel pain and now I have delivered more pain and you are in my mind all the time as you go through this. In that way you are very close to me, even being so far away.

My sincerest and deepest love to you all. And thank you, dearest sister, for being the listener.

Frank

~~~

Richard-Symons was in his 50s. He had been educated at what was considered to be the foremost academic school in his city and served an apprenticeship as stationer and publisher at a very respectable firm, with which he remained after his apprenticeship, in due course becoming a director and subsequently the managing director and finally the owner of the establishment. Though in his youth his appearance may have been that of a young man acquainted with the more carefree pleasure-seeking stratum of his peer-group - if you had met him your impression might even have been 'jaunty' - he had approached the transition to adulthood in a sober and responsible manner, to the relief - and slight surprise - of his father, Richard. So the man who disembarked from the SS Saxon in East London on 25th July 1902 was unmistakably an established and successful English man of affairs. He had certainly relinquished the somewhat *laissez-faire* approach of his youth and now saw himself as someone who took a meticulously calculated view of life and business and how it should be conducted. You could say he had a vision of his place in the world, and he made decisions which kept him in step with this vision. Thus his bearing was that of confident 'man of the world', even though in his 56 years he had never actually travelled beyond England itself. Neither in his 56 years had he encountered such a dislocation of culture and life circumstances as awaited him when he set foot on African soil.

Frank was there on the quayside, as he promised he would be, only a few yards along the jetty from where the cutter brought them in, and he was smiling, not with joy but with greeting... but he was not coming over. The porter had put down his luggage and was waiting, and for an instant Richard-Symons was lost in the space which time makes when we lose our place in the script. That was the moment he saw the crutch which Frank was leaning on and the loosely-hanging trouser fabric from where his left knee... Where was his shoe? The realisation came slowly, the few steps he took to reach him could have been crossing a chasm. And then he was holding him. "My God what has happened?"

"So much, Father, so much more than you could ever imagine."

How many seconds, how many minutes? There were no words. Time stopped. And then Richard-Symons felt his self-control slowly slipping and he did something he could not ever remember doing. He cried. How long? Who knows?

For Frank, relief, amazement - was this really his father? - compassion, tenderness... somewhere wondering about Nobomi who had been standing behind his father and was not yet in his awareness. Then he saw she was telling the porter to wait, and the movement caught his father's attention and pulled him slightly out of his grief, enough to turn his head questioning, but Frank; "It's alright, Father, she is with us, I will introduce you when you are ready." For

Richard-Symons, reassurance for a moment, but bewilderment. He looked Frank in the face, a look of complete incomprehension, then turned to look at Nobomi, "Who are you?"

"I am Nobomi. I am... I was Harry's girlfriend."

He looked back to Frank, his shoulders drooping, his head bowed, as Frank had never before seen him. "I am lost, Frank. I need to lie down. Take me to the hotel."

Nobomi had managed to secure a car, which was now also waiting; slowly the party mounted and finally set off for the Beach Hotel.

conversations… 2

<u>*Letter from Barbara to Louie 21st July 1948*</u>

Dear Aunt Louie

I hope you are keeping well, because it seems a very long time since I have seen you. I hear that you have moved into your own flat, so I am not going to ask about Aunt Jenifer and Aunt Nora because you won't be seeing os much of them, but I am sure that you would let me know if any of you needed anything.

As you know Norman and I moved into our own place finally. It is not far from Mother, who is very pleased we have found somewhere on this side of town. (I think I would not mind if it had been a little further away on this side of town, but I trust you not to tell her I said that.) It is quite quiet and there is some garden for me to potter in.

This enquiry will probably seem to come out of the blue, but I am wondering whether you can help me with something, because you seem to be the custodian of family history and secrets. I would like to know about the uncle we had that nobody has ever talked about. I can't remember when I first discovered he existed or how, except that I asked Mother and all she said was that it was only for Father to talk about. Not helpful because Father had already died and so had Grandfather. So I am stuck. It has come up because Peter mentioned him in a letter à propos something else, but he doesn't know any more than I do. Except he did know his name was Harry. So if you can spare us some of your little gems, we would be very pleased.

Anyway, are you going back to the Salzburg festival this year? I was always very admiring of the way you toddled off by train all on your own. If you are, I hope you have a wonderful time wallowing in the music and the scenery. Do you go to Salzburg via Vienna? My geography is not very good, is it?

All love and good wishes,

Barbara

~~~

They were sitting in the lounge of the hotel, just Frank and his father. Frank was staying in the hotel again to be near his father, a concession from the manager who now considered him respectable enough in the company of his father. Nobomi had returned to Fitzpatrick Road the evening Richard-Symons had arrived. For her the hotel was not welcoming, even though Frank had not reported to her the earlier pomposity and snobbery of the management, though he clearly indicated to her his own disdain for those individuals. But Nobomi found the atmosphere intimidating.

It was the second day after his father's arrival. The previous day Richard-Symons had barely left his room and had spent a long time trying to compose his thoughts, with the aid of the journal which he had kept for many years, then starting a letter to Fanny, setting it aside several times, finally abandoning it and returning to his journal pondering. He had probably done some reading, though he could not remember what, and he must have eaten at some point, though he had no recollection of any meals or even where he ate them. There was something unsettled and unsettling deep down inside him, something resonating (though not with a harmonious tone), a deep disturbing discord. It had been with him all day yesterday and was still there, though less intrusive at this moment. He could have given himself the facile explanation that, of course, what did he expect after the cataclysms of Harry's death and Frank's leg, but he knew that there was something else. Something more existential. Perhaps it was to do with the fact that he was on this African continent. Not the first time for their family: but even though he knew family tradition and newspaper reports held that his elder uncle (whom he had never seen) was lost in Africa having gone in search of a certain "black queen" and even speculated that he had found and married her, he himself had never even crossed the English Channel. On occasions he knew he could be swept up in the popular fervour about the Empire - patriotic, not jingoistic, he would be quick to say - and could catch himself daydreaming of vast open spaces under another sun, free from the clutter and introspective preoccupations of his normal routine. Now here he was, under another sun, but this place and what he found here, far from offering relief, seemed to demand that he abandon all that he thought he knew and look on without even trying to work things out, because anyway he could have no real understanding...

"Can I bring you gentlemen some coffee?". The waiter was at their side. "You could take it here or on the terrace, if you would prefer."

There's another incongruity, he thought - suddenly it's like the Pump Rooms in elegant Bath, where he and Fanny...

Frank answered, "We are fine here, thank you."

And Frank, he seems so... normal.

"Does it hurt?"

"Not often now. If I hit something unexpectedly. Sometimes it aches in the night, and I cannot work out where the ache is." Then: "There are many worse than me, arms, legs, whole legs. The Boers had a massive canon called Long Tom. But it was as often as not the infections that led to amputations. The surgeon told me. Out in the field gangrene is almost inevitable."

Then after a pause: "But I did not want to be a soldier. I was support. I wanted to do what gave our guys - the real soldiers - the best chance."

And again: "In a war everyone thinks they are right. And if they believe they are also the stronger and will win, that's when the worst destruction happens. But nobody wins. They signed a peace treaty 3 months ago and the Boers will have their own States in the Empire, self-governing of course as they wanted, and we are helping them to get their farms working again. We are giving them money to re-start, and I am not against that. And the Afrikaans, they will still be able to get men, African men, Indian men, Chinese men, and some Europeans - but they have to pay more for Europeans - to go down the mines. The best for this country would be if no-one believed they had an advantage and could come out on top. Then there would be no point in competition, would there? there could be cooperation. But that's being simplistic. In a few years time, who will it be that believes they have the right to be in control?"

Richard-Symons recalled his conversations with Isabella on the SS Saxon after dinner, and something troubled him, he knew, but he couldn't quite put the right words to it... everyone was acting as if the land, this land, belonged to them. The Empire, the Boers, the Afrikaans, they all wanted their bit, but did all these interests really have to clash, after all this was a very big country... and then, weren't there people here to begin with? but not the Africans who were the majority now, Isabella had said, *they* mostly came from further north and they had invaded too... and even Isabella, she hadn't taken sides like in a war, she was here to relieve suffering, he believed that, but even she seemed to be mostly taking care of the Boers in the camps, when there were native camps even worse off right alongside...

He wondered what Harry had made of it all. Yes, Harry, he needed to know more about Harry...

"Would you have been with him that evening, if it hadn't been for your leg, Frank?"

"It is possible, yes, but we each had our own lives, Father. Swimming was natural for Harry in a way it never was for me. I think it was the exhilaration of being carried along on a course without boundaries. But we were different. I am an engineer and for me, being able to define something, knowing where the edges are, is vital. So he had his own life, but I saw him regularly. He was really settled in."

"With Nobomi?"

"Yes, with Nobomi. They were getting on really well, you could tell that somehow, in spite of all the differences between them, they were good for each other." He paused. "And there is something else, Father, you need to know. Nobomi is pregnant."

Now his head was swimming again. The ground had just given way. The room around them some other scene. All connection with real life seemed to have vanished. Images of Fanny, the girls at home, his office and the printing works, all floating free, unanchored on a vast uncharted deep.

"Harry?"

"Yes, Harry. They were in love."

"This place, it feels so foreign, Frank."

~~~

"Harry, wake up, wake up."

She was kneeling on the bed half-dressed. "Harry please, please, wake up. I must tell you something."

Light filtered through slowly. Should he be at work? No, not this Saturday. We went down to the bar last night, so it couldn't be today.

"I'm pregnant."

"It's too early."

"Wake up. We are going to have a baby."

"Whose baby?"

"Our baby. You and me."

Now he saw her, a smiling face looking down, as he rolled onto his back, realising he was held fast by her arms either side of his head, her hands planted firmly on the pillow.

"I knew this morning. I woke up early. It was there. We know these things. I am Xhosa."

~~~

"She is black. She is a native." Richard-Symons was not really conscious of whether he had said the words aloud or whether they were just in his head.

"It will be your first grandchild."

"But these things don't happen, Frank. Not to us."

"There are many coloureds here. Peoples have moved around Africa for thousands of years. And not all of them what you call black. There are different nations of native people and then there are Indians and Chinese and Europeans."

"But that's Africa."

"We are in Africa, Father. We are in their land."

After a long pause his father turned to look him in the face: "Won't it be difficult, Frank? What will I tell your mother?"

"Mother will know already. I wrote to Louie while you were on your way."

"But Frank, we didn't need to tell any…" His voice trailed off as he realised the absurdity and vanity in what he was going to say. He bowed his head, "I'm sorry."

~~~

"Don't worry, I will go to one of your doctors and they will say, yes, I am pregnant, but we have people who know these things as well and I will find a Xhosa woman to help me and she will introduce me to an elder here in East London, perhaps there is someone from my father's *Ama* and they will tell me what we have to do and what you have to do, Harry, you have to speak to my father, you have to pay him because we are not married and then it is accepted... will you send a message today, Harry?"

"Harry?"

Harry's unfocused gaze might have been looking at her, but for the first time that he could remember, there seemed to be no next thing waiting, and his sense of life always moving on and of he himself taking what came and letting it be who he was, all of his letting and doing and floating with where his life went, all this was at a standstill. No sound reached him now in the shadowy stillness of the room.

"I am happy, Harry, and my family will be happy and my father, he knew, he understood, he told me - Ewe, hamba, uyazulazula, ndiyaqonda - yes, walk, wanderer, I understand. You are wanderer too, Harry. Your ancestors, perhaps they were wanderers. Our child will have blood from both mfengu."

Harry thought of his father, who had turned away so quickly that last day, as if he could not bear to witness his leaving. It was not that he had lost the excitement that it had brought, the breaking away from the life that had been set out for him; he had settled here, it suited him, and he had a wonderful girl whom he loved, yes, really loved... so what was it? was he scared? was all his carefree jaunty devil-may-care approach to life just a sham? when he was really tested? - Is that it? I am scared? - He suddenly saw himself as dishonest. That was uncomfortable. He wished his father were there, and that was not something that had ever come to him before. Should he talk to Frank? Frank was like his father in some ways, so perhaps...

"Lie down with me, *umntu wam*, I need you and I will be good to you."

~~~

"Tell me how this is going to work, Frank."

"We can do things when you are ready, Father. We will go to the Council Offices and they will give you a certificate for Harry's burial which will have the number of his grave and then we will be able to arrange a memorial. There is a charge, but it will not be very much. I will take you there, Father, and we can stay as long as you want and when you are ready we will come back and just be here quietly."

Perhaps he was seeing his imagined version of the scenes as Frank spoke, but if he was, the characters

conversations... 2

were moving mute on a darkened stage, for his face showed no sign that he was following what was playing out, no sign yet that he knew he also had a part in the script. His mind was producing random thoughts, unrelated arguments and half-formed questions...

"I should talk to Nobomi."

"Of course, Father, when you are ready. She will want to talk to you."

"Where is she? Is she here?"

"She lives in Harry's room, not far away."

"Why did he not tell me?"

"I don't know."

"But you knew. You could have told me."

Frank could feel the conversation shifting towards difficult terrain, but equally knew his father was following his own course, however winding it might be.

"When is the baby?"

"About 6 months."

"I will be away a long time." Then "Does she want to have a baby? Couldn't she...? I would pay."

Frank's stomach turned. "Yes, she does, Father. She is Xhosa. I will tell you about what that means when we have done the right things for Harry."

"Perhaps Isabella can help."

"Who is Isabella?"

"Isabella? She is… who is Isabella?… later…I think I have to go slowly."

~~~

Letter from Louie to Barbara 1st August 1948

Dear Barbara,

I was so pleased to get your letter. It was lucky that I had thought to send your mother my new address quickly, or it would have been some while before I saw it. At the moment it is quite difficult for Nora and Jenifer to come across here, now that I have moved into my little flat. I am on the other side of town, you know.

But enough of that, I am glad to hear that you and Norman are settled in now in your new flat and I hope you will be very comfortable there. I would love to come up and visit all of you in Bristol, but you know August is quite busy for me. Yes, I am going to the Salzburg festival again this year. I used to go before the war, as you know, and I really wanted to go again now that Austria is free. (They never stopped the *festival during the War, you know. Important propaganda for the Nazis, I suppose.) I am going as I always did by train of course and it will take 2 days.*

You asked me about your uncle Harry, who died in South Africa, but first I must tell you that I don't know everything. I was the youngest (apart from Harry of course) and I am sure I was never given the full story, not by Father - well that's not surprising - but not by <u>your</u> father either and he and I were always close, so I was cross when I thought he was hiding things and I used to nag him to tell me more. But it didn't do any good of course. He was quite like Father really.

So, what I remember is that Frank (your father) went to Cape Colony the year he was 21 because he wanted to expand his opportunities. I think he and Father had a row about it because Father wanted him to go into the firm, but Frank was not interested in publishing and printing, he was an engineering type. (You know that of course, don't you.)

So Frank went and seemed to get himself established, and about a year afterwards

Harry wanted to go. Well _that_ almost started a war. Harry was the darling of Mother and I always thought Father too (though he didn't always show it), I suppose it was because he was the youngest. Harry wrote to Frank and Frank replied that he could set him up with a job - he was only just 17 - and he ought to come. Father did not like that at all. But anyway, he went, and Frank _had_ got him a job, so Mother felt a little relieved. Then Frank disappeared, at least he didn't write for months and months and all we got from Harry was short notes in his usual happy-go-lucky style. But one morning a telegram arrived from Frank saying that Harry had drowned. I can't describe that morning. I can still hear the screaming. I remember I had to go out. I could hear the crying behind me as I walked up the street. It was awful.

This is where it starts to get hazy, even though Frank wrote to me. I seem to have lost his letters, I am sorry Barbara. Father went out to South Africa, as you would expect, and he was away a very long time, almost a year I think. When he arrived he found Frank had lost most of one leg. But *at home we already knew because Frank had written to me while Father was on his way. It was in the fighting, because he had joined some Cyclist Corps who supported the troops, but they got into the middle of a battle I think.*

So Father landed there - it was a port called East London - to give his youngest son a proper burial and found his second son crippled. This is where it gets really hazy, because I cannot remember what came from Father and what came from Frank and as I said I do not believe either of them told me everything, but there was talk of an African girl and a Quaker nurse and Harry had a child. I remember my mother, just before she died, told me she was sorry that she could not give me the locket her mother had given her, because she had given it to the African girl who was Harry's girlfriend. I knew that anyway because I had sent it for her. Mother could not remember her name, but I remember it, it was Nobomi.

That is all I can tell you. I am so sorry I am missing so much and I wish I could find

Frank's letters, but I hope that much helps you.

I hope you are recovering now from your hard times in the War. You did a wonderful job. It must have been very frightening driving out while the bombs were falling. I admire you Barbara.

I will send you a postcard from Salzburg if I can find any.

With loving good wishes,

Louie

ps. you'll never believe, but after I finished writing to you I did some rummaging in boxes I had forgotten about for years, and I found this photograph - it must be Harry's African girlfriend - I could not believe my eyes when I found it. I am so pleased. You can keep it now because I know you take care of family things.

~~~

<u>Letter from Barbara to Hugh 30th August 1948</u>

Dear Hugh,

Thank you for your very thoughtful letter in reply to all my philosophising. You really didn't need to be so concerned about my breaking off in the middle, you have far more important things to be concerned about than my silly preoccupations. I think it was when I brought in the family stuff, family is a bit of a thing with us and it must be a kind of trigger for me. I thought we would be able to start a family, Norman and I, as soon as the War was over, but it hasn't happened and I've been panicking a bit lately. And then you know how you get silly thoughts coming into your mind, like I've got 3 maiden aunts and what have their lives been like being childless. Perhaps one of them didn't mind because she was a head-mistress, but you know what I mean. No, you probably don't know what I mean, because you are a man. I think Peter knows what I mean, but it might be easier for him because he's... well, just because. And he's so come day go day and easy-going. I think you've got the easy-going bit too, Hugh, but maybe you disagree.

Sorry this is short. I just wanted to say don't worry, and I have to go now. I will write again soon, I promise.

Go safely,

Barbara

White Cat

~~~

They were sitting one evening on the grass verge which separates the Esplanade from the rocky foreshore of the ocean. Sometimes, when they had eaten, they would go to the bar in Fitzpatrick Road, but it depended who was in because occasionally there was an atmosphere: then the whole room hushed when they arrived. It was widely known now that Nobomi was pregnant and he was the father. Was he "white man" and "Empire"? But that wouldn't ring true surely, because if that were him and he acted that out, he would have just walked away by now. So more often they came here to the Esplanade and looked for a place without people, where the only sounds would be the muted thud of the waves and pebbles rattling down the shore as the next wave began.

It was Nobomi who spoke first.

"Do not be afraid, *umntu wam*. There are others like us and my father is a good man. My clan will welcome you. There are things to do with a birth and because we are not married, to respect my family and respect our clan. But then we will be accepted with our child."

"I feel very young, *sthandwa sam*. You left your home to join the rest of the world. I came here to have an adventure with my brother but I did not really leave my family home at all. You have become a woman, but I don't think I have become a man yet."

"In our clan you would be learning now to be a man. There is ulwaluko, which is initiation, and you spend many days with elders. Then you are ready and everyone knows you are a man. Then *you* know you are a man."

"I have not made myself ready."

"You must be ready to be a father."

"Your people have wisdom in their ways. We do not have the same rituals and I feel unprepared. I think it will be a long time before I gain your wisdom." He paused. "I wish I could know how I can feel so close to you in my heart and so far away in the turmoil of my mind. There seems so little time."

"You took me in that night. You made yourself the one. Please stay with me now."

It was almost dark, the waves' sound no more than a gentle lapping. They walked slowly home.

~~~

Author's journal 10th December 2021:

I lingered a long time over the circumstances of Harry's death. It would have been easy to conclude that it was suicide. The sea wasn't completely calm (but he was a strong swimmer and by this time knew the waters off East London well); he was a young man with limited life experience confronted by circumstances for which he had no axiom to guide him (but all his life he had been his own motivator, happy to find his way along unknown paths); in prospect was a life-change which was certain to bring dislocating cultural differences (but he had no doubt of Nobomi's love and her belief in their child); his child's mother was attached to her roots and South Africa was a developing country riven with competing economic and political factions and with no obvious haven of stability for a young family (though surely in such a large country it would always be possible for an adaptable loving father to steer a safe course for his family)... no, in the end I did not believe it was pre-meditated suicide, though all of those unpropitious factors, I was sure, played a part in his death.

Drowning is a slow death, and the realisation of there being no escape, comes gradually. The moment when the struggle is relinquished cannot be identified with a specific physical state, rather it is the mind which says, "I cannot... any longer", and that point is not pre-determined, but is affected by the mind's sense of its own resilience in the face of all that is up against it, or might be up against it.

I did not believe that Harry voluntarily gave up his family, past or future, but that his strength to fight against the odds was fatally compromised when it mattered most.

passing through

Extract from the obituary in 1957 for Isabella Davy in the archives of Ackworth School near Pontefract:

"…She went to South Africa during the Boer War, on behalf of the Society of Friends, to nurse for most of 1902 among the Boers interned in British concentration camps. The "devotion to her unattractive patients" which a camp commandant noted in his testimonial was surely no more than her deep natural sympathy for her fellow-men. Most of her subsequent life was spent as a private maternity nurse… She also nursed at Ackworth during the great influenza epidemic of 1918, and undertook relief work for the Society of Friends in Vienna in 1919 and 1921… so great was her gift for entering into the lives of others that her life soon became filled with personal friendships… "Such a Grand old Lady" wrote [one] on hearing of Isabella Davy's death…"

~~~

It was on 3rd October 1902 that Richard-Symons finally went with Frank to the Town Office of East London and received the "Certificate of Ownership of Grave Space". Harry's name does not appear on the certificate which records his grave as, "being Lot No. 592.5C in the New Cemetery, East London on the East Bank of the Buffalo River."

~~~

A few days after he had arrived, Richard-Symons returned to the Beach Hotel from a more than usually lengthy morning walk and was given a telephone message by the manager to the effect that a Miss Isabella Davy had called and had asked that he be informed that she would return around 6 that evening and hope to be able to see him. His heart missed a beat, he was sure, and then felt lighter. He went straight to his room to collect his thoughts.

Isabella knew nothing of Nobomi, nor a future grandchild, nor Frank's leg, for he had known none of those things while they were on the ship. Somehow he would have to tell her all of this, without sounding incomprehensible. What brought more pressure and a little nervousness was that he had never got to the point of telling Frank about Isabella, which he would now have to do, and quickly, for it was normal to meet Frank for dinner each evening.

"The Isabella that I mentioned in connection with my voyage here," he was telling Frank when he had arrived back at the hotel, "is a nurse sent by the Society of Friends to help in the concentration camps. She was a great help to me as I was trying to prepare for arriving here. She had said she would try to contact me before she left to go on to her destination north, near Johannesburg I think. She is coming here this evening. There was a message. Perhaps she will be in time to join us for dinner. Do you think that would be alright? I feel... it all feels, rather strange... this person from outside looking in on our family... but I am not sure what our family is any longer. I shall need your help, Frank."

They had eaten dinner the three of them, after Isabella arrived, and Frank had held the conversation together in the way that he always could, filling in details of family and circumstances and events which now, now that they were looking back at them, seemed like a winding path across an open moor, a path that was always there - you could tell if you glanced behind you - but suddenly was brought into relief with the changing light. Such are those places where walkers discover themselves standing in open space from which no clear way seems to lead except the way they came. Looking down the turf is lush and vivid green and interspersed with dark gullies for you are standing on an upland reservoir and from here all flows outwards. This was the sense of watershed that recounting events gave for both men.

"I would like to meet Nobomi."

Isabella's sudden interjection brought the mens' thoughts back into the room.

"...if you were agreeable and if it were not an intrusion."

For Frank and Richard-Symons it was far from that, indeed it was a relief, for both felt themselves at a loss and saw no obvious way to move forward, their sense of responsibility and their own inexperience nagging constantly in their minds. But Richard-Symons had not yet visited 45 Fitzpatrick Road, where Nobomi was now living and this evening he again demurred, so it was Frank and Isabella who set out for Harry's former lodgings. Slightly hesitantly Frank mounted the staircase to the outside corridor and, perhaps even apologetically, knocked on the door. Nobomi answered, her face solemn and drawn, but her eyes slightly brightening on seeing Frank. She let them in without a word and all three sat where they could in the rather dishevelled room. Isabella smiled and introduced herself while Frank was still wondering how he would start.

"I met Harry's father on the ship and he was a good companion during the voyage. He told me about what happened to Harry and I am so sorry for all of you for this tragedy. I would like to be some help somehow if that were possible, you see, I am a nurse, I take care of people who are ill, and I take care of women when they give birth. I have a religion which says that I must be a friend for anyone who needs me."

Nobomi seemed to be looking somewhere beyond the dingy room. Frank noticed that she was wearing the locket round her neck and was clutching the pendant firmly with her left hand across her chest. There was a long silence before Isabella spoke again:

"I shall be in East London for a while because I am working here in the camp. Could I come and visit you again? We could talk about Harry and about your baby."

Nobomi looked down and nodded.

"Could I make you a drink now and then you can tell us if you want us to go?"

Again Nobomi nodded.

Frank felt oddly perplexed. He knew he was relieved that Isabella was handling the emotional circumstances in which they found themselves (and which seemed worse than he was used to - though he visited each day), but he also felt regret, for he had grown to genuinely like Nobomi and with his young Englishman's sense of honour wanted to be the one to offer whatever support was needed.

They left shortly afterwards and returned to Richard-Symons, who was waiting for them apprehensively. "She is suffering with melancholia" was how Isabella described Nobomi's state. "She is bearing the death of her child's father and she is a long way from home. Though her people are all around her here, she seems very nervous and only wants to stay inside." "I would like to try to help her and I could have the time, now that they want me to stay in East London for the moment. But we should talk, Richard, about what you can offer to the child when it is born and where might be the right place for mother and child to live. I am not very knowledgeable about this country, but there are Friends with whom I can talk, without giving names or making difficulties, I give you my assurance on that." Isabella's practised professional manner was a welcome solace.

"Thank you. I am most grateful."

White Cat

~~~

Letter from Louie to Barbara 4th September 1948

Dear Barbara

I had a wonderful time in Salzburg and I would love to be able to show you some of my photographs - I still use my little box camera - but better still of course was the music, and unfortunately I am not able to share that with you. But never mind.

I love long train journeys as well. They give you the benefit of two new worlds together, there is the countryside that is going past outside and then there are all the people on the train with you. Of course it can get a little difficult sometimes with so many people talking around you, but I am a bit of a chatterbox myself. You asked if you go through Vienna to get to Salzburg. Well the answer is no, but this time I went down through Germany instead of France because I thought I would this once spend a night in Vienna. I could have changed at Linz because you have to come back through there, but I decided to stay on, and I am very pleased that I did because I travelled with a very nice man on the train *from Vienna. In other ways I was sorry that I had gone to Vienna because it has been so damaged by the War and it has not yet been rebuilt. The are still piles of stones and rubble from the bombing all over and there are even people living in places they have dug out among the ruins, and children just wandering around, poor things. I think the soldiers are trying to keep them safe and get them to the authorities, but there is not enough money for proper care and there are so many of them of all ages. I almost fell over one in Stephans Platz, I wasn't looking where I was going, I think I was walking backwards to take a better picture of the cathedral and she was picking something up from the ground and she was African and I was so surprised to see an African girl in Vienna, but she ran off very quickly, so I think I must have scared her.*

Anyway, back to my conversation with this charming man in the train, who was a soldier, though he wasn't in uniform, which he <u>half</u> explained to me, but I am not sure that I completely believed him - you know I have an intuition about men not telling you everything, like Frank and Father, do you remember? He was a music lover, he *told me, and he was hoping that they would finish the rebuilding of the Opera before his duty ended in Vienna, because they were putting it back to how it was before the fire and he had been told it was magnificent. He said it was quite a coincidence when he was sent to Vienna because his father had been conscripted at the end of the 1914-18 war and had been sent to Vienna and had found himself working with three Quaker women who were doing relief work distributing donations from England. He remembered because they were all from the same school, somewhere near Pontefract, I think. His father said it was a good education in the facts of life because one of them was a nurse and she did everything from delivering babies to de-lousing hair! Oh dear, I'm rambling again. Such a chatterbox. But my soldier companion was wanting me to contribute to his life education in romantic matters of all things - me, can you imagine, a spinster all my life, although not really out of choice - anyway, he said there was a young woman he had met completely by chance when he was on leave in England and he wanted to send her something that would appeal to her because he had no idea when he might be able to get back. He was wondering if one of the Augarten white porcelain pieces would please, they had a rather attractive cat. I told him that I was not the best person to ask, but I would like it, if it was me. He told me about what they were doing as well, his unit, and a lot of it seems to have been what his father had been doing after the last war, looking out for the children. Life is strange isn't it, the way it winds around? Then I bumped into him again on the platform on Salzburg station as I was leaving to come home. Don't you think that was odd? when he had not said that he was also coming to Salzburg? because he had got off at Graz?*

With all this chattering, I almost forgot the main reason why I was writing. When I got home from Salzburg, something was nagging on my mind, and I just could not work out what it was. But it was like my trip had activated a dim memory. Anyway I did some more rummaging and found the certificate for Harry's burial in East London which I am sending with this letter. Would you ever go to South Africa? No, it is rather a long way. I think I am a bit too old now. But I was also rummaging in my head and I remembered the name of the Quaker nurse, whom father had met on the ship and who looked after Harry's girlfriend when she had her baby. I'm sure her name was Isabella. I think it stuck in my mind because it was slightly unusual.

And that is not quite all. I have found a letter from our mother to Harry. It was in the secret compartment of the campaign writing slope that Father used. I had tried several times to get into this compartment and not succeeded, but then I thought to ask an antique dealer in town and he told me how to do it. (They were quite common apparently.) Anyway, that doesn't completely solve the mystery, because the letter seems to be an answer which Mother sent to a letter Harry had sent to her. So why did Father have it? I can only think that it arrived too late and it was amongst Harry's things that Father brought back, because it was still in the envelope unopened. Father must have put it away and forgotten about it. Or perhaps he put it away so that it didn't hurt Mother to know Harry had never seen it. Anyway, I am not sending the letter to you because there are one or two things which are very personal and I think we should all be dead before they come out. So, I am going to copy out the parts that might help you.

Here they are:

..."I know you are torn, my son, and I wish I could be there to help you and talk to you both, you and Nobomi. It is in my nature to say that love is the most important thing <u>always</u>, because it brings us closest to the person that we truly are. In each and every moment I believe that is true. But I have wondered over the years whether we can say that as an absolute truth when we have to allow for what might happen as time moves on, and when people, all sorts of people, affect what happens in our lives. Your father would have a business man's way of sorting it out - I know that his nature is different to yours and, in many ways, to mine as well, but there is usually merit in the practical way he looks at things. I think he would say something like this: - make a list of the people who matter most and who are affected by what you are wanting to decide (and the list <u>must</u> include yourself);

then add up for each of them the cost to <u>them</u> if you decide this way or that way or the other way; then add everybody's costs for each of your ways together and see which way costs the least.

Now I will add my part to your father's method, as it might apply to you in what you have asked me. It is this: there are only 3 people you should consider in this and they are Nobomi, yourself and your child not yet born. <u>We</u> do not matter, your father, me, your brothers and sisters, the Church, our society, the business. What you decide must be what is important <u>only</u> for the three of you. Listen to the God within you, my son"...

That was it. It made it all so real, when I read it. It was as if I was back there again and they were all around me. 50 years ago.

Aren't I a sentimental silly? But as soon as I read it, I wanted to pass her thoughts on to someone, and you are obviously the right person. There have been some good women in our family. I will tell you more sometime.

With loving good wishes,
Louie

~~~

Author's journal 11th December 2021:

It occurs to me how, 50 years on, Barbara's struggle with her situation was in some ways a mirror image of Harry's. Both involved children unborn, both involved a pull between love and 'duty', though duty in a not very exalted sense, more like the expectations of others - society, family, school, other people's ideas about how they should behave, and both involved misadventure - in Harry's case personal tragedy, but at the moment I cannot tell how to construe the outcome for Barbara. There are two other salient aspects which are interesting. Both of them had a confidant, for Harry it was his mother Fanny, for Barbara it was her younger brother Peter, and both of those were of a similar 'nature' (we would probably say character or personality or even philosophy now, but Fanny and Richard-Symons seemed to use 'nature'). And then the other aspect: of Frank's generation four out of six had no children; in Barbara's generation three out of four had no children.

~~~

Letter from Hugh to Barbara 17th September 1948

Dear Barbara

I hope you don't consider this forward or inappropriate, but I saw this figurine in a shop in a rather nice part of the city the other day. It is the white porcelain for which Vienna is famous. I wander around when I get the chance, because Vienna is/was (but will be again) such a magnificent city and you find such interesting things in all sorts of nooks and crannies. I wasn't looking for something to get you, honestly - no, not honestly, that's a lie - but this wonderful cat just leapt out at me, well, almost, it was actually sitting, as you see. I've put in the card of the shop where I bought it. I nearly didn't go in because the things in the main shop were rather garishly painted - not my taste and I was fairly sure not your's either - but then you could go through a door and there was another room, a bit smaller, quite dark, except that on individual shelves mounted randomly all over the walls were pure white figurines, mainly animals. They shone and seemed to sparkle like stars on the dark blue walls, and amongst them was this cat and I decided there and then you must have it.

I haven't given it a name. I don't know whether it's a boy or a girl! I hope it doesn't have to hide for too long before it can come out into the light. I hope I shall see it again soon.

And you.

Hugh

<u>Letter from Barbara to Peter 30th September 1948</u>

Oh brother... HELP!

He's sending me presents. A white cat in Viennese porcelain. What do I do?

Come on, Barbara, keep things in perspective, he's sent you <u>one</u> present. Just because he liked the cat, and he's got no-one else to buy it for, so he sent it to you.

Why didn't he send it to his mother? Or his sister? Has he really got a mother or a sister? You don't know anything about him.

Peter, you said there were lots of spies in Vienna. Could he be a spy? It stuck in my mind the way he slashed the tyre of my bicycle that first evening. It was so quick, a sudden gash, and the knife as well, it just appeared, the blade snapped out and then it was gone again. I didn't see where it came from.

And to make matters worse, Louie has met him! Tell me it's impossible. But she has. She doesn't know she's met him. She doesn't know there's a him to meet, but she has, on a train from Vienna to Salzburg when she was on her way to the Salzburg festival. We had been corresponding on family and heirloom things and she wrote to me when she got back and told me all about this lovely soldier she was talking to on the train - you know what a chatterbox she is - and he asked her whether he should buy this white porcelain cat he had seen for a girl he had met quite by chance on his last leave in England. That must have been me!

And it gets worse. He said he was a soldier, an officer, but he wasn't in uniform. She didn't completely believe him. She says she has an intuition about men not telling you everything.

I don't know why I am writing to you. You can't get a letter to me before I have to write to Hugh... and thank him! But there's no-one else I would talk to. The most likely would be Louie. There's an irony. But she is so strict on morals and she would be suspicious immediately and then she would never speak to me again. Of course, the most level-headed person around is Norman! There's another irony.

Thank you for reading all this. I hope all is well with you.

Your <u>very</u> appreciative sister,

<u>Barbara</u>

~~~

Over the next few weeks Nobomi received two visitors most days. Frank continued to call every day as he had since he moved into the hotel to be with his father; Isabella called separately, announcing herself in her professional capacity as nurse and usually stayed to talk for at least an hour. Nobomi had let go of her early excitement over her own people's methods and practices around childbirth and simply accepted the English nurse as her guide. This was more from the fatigue and lethargy that came with her melancholia than any betrayal of her roots, though Isabella continued to be perplexed by her extreme nervousness about any contact with her own people, who were numerous in East London. But when Frank disclosed the circumstances of Nobomi's arrival in the middle of the night at 45 Fitzpatrick Road, she was able to put together a more complete picture. Frank's information, though, was both a relief (because she could account better for her patient's condition) and a concern, because it could complicate whatever arrangements might be able to be made for the future of mother and baby, and Richard-Symons' collaboration. It also closed a door which might have offered wider contact for Nobomi and the possibility of re-introducing her to her own people through the camp in East London, for, whilst the camp mostly housed Boer women and children it also had two huts where native African women (she had hoped Xhosa, though she was not sure) were living. And now, suddenly, time did not seem to be on their side, for the East London camp was supposed to be closing before the end of the year, at which point Isabella herself would be expected to move to the camp at Kronstaadt, a long way distant, beyond the Xhosa homeland.

Towards the end of August, Isabella was becoming troubled. She retired to bed late and rose early, neither of which were unknown to her, but this time she was feeling a lack of the renewal of energy and spirit which usually supported her during periods of heavy duties. She realised that she was struggling with the complications of her different and often conflicting supporting roles. Foremost of course was her patient, but the need to keep on terms with Frank and his father, both of whom were trying to resolve their places and their own roles in the unfolding drama, but whom she knew to be vital for their financial means. She liked Frank for the way he had not hesitated in picking up Nobomi and for diligently and selflessly caring for her since the fateful discovery of Harry's death. Her heart went out to Richard-Symons, whose world had been overturned by events and who had no model for another, nor a faith like hers to trust that a way would always appear. But was she not also floundering a little herself?

Instinctively Isabella knew that the child must be with its mother, but it would be a 'coloured', and with a mother not versed in the ways of the town, whether or not she could find kin nearby; a mother who had so recently been awakened to the iniquities of human nature and felt disillusion that she could be so violated even by her own people.

And there would be more to come. The colony was well used to its confusion of nation and tribe and clan within an assortment of races, to affiliations and alliances which shifted according to convenience, whether that be political or financial or personal (the war had merely brought these into sharper relief), and already in the background hovered the spectre of degrading segregation by race, native and European, white and black and Asian. This place, East London, was leading that sad cortège, having been the product largely of military expansion which facilitated a social structure around supply and commerce, and a coincidental class distinction along ethnic lines.

In all this, on a personal level, custom and ritual could not be ignored: if it were even possible to return Nobomi to her homeland, some 200 miles distant, her acceptance with her child would depend on payment to her father by Richard-Symons of the appropriate damages required by Xhosa culture.

Isabella had a sense of all their sufferings and knew that the time available for Nobomi, now pregnant for at least 4 months, to undertake the hazardous journey back to Matatiele, was very limited.

And surely, we should ask Nobomi herself?

~~~

It was the first time, since Frank had brought Isabella to introduce her to Nobomi, that they had both visited her together.

Frank began: "We have come to talk about what will happen when you have your baby. We want you to be safe and to be able to live with your baby somewhere that can be your home."

"I cannot go back to my family, it is a very long way and I will not be accepted. I need to be with a man, but no man of my people would accept me now. Harry is my man. My clan will not support me."

The answer took both Frank and Isabella off-guard: they had been sure that returning the mother to her own people with sufficient financial compensation and support would be the most humane solution. The tone in her voice also caused them concern, for there was no hint of defiance or challenge, no, more worryingly, her voice was expressionless and seemed to come from the emptiness of a hopeless resignation. Frank realised that if at that moment she had been told she could not remain at 45 Fitzpatrick Road, which had become her home, she would simply have gathered her few possessions and left; she would not look back, and they would watch as she disappeared into the night.

They had been there only a few minutes and already Frank felt ill-prepared. Not that he had had no plan - the plan had been to return Nobomi to her family while there was still the time, or to find kin closer to hand - the engineer in him had determined the objective and would assemble the means needed. But what now faced him was not anything that could be resolved by a design applied from outside to achieve a pre-determined solution. He was deflated. For all they had only just begun, he needed time to think, perhaps time to talk again to his father. He excused himself, asking Isabella to stay until he returned - and he promised to return - later in the evening. As he left she said quietly to him, "we cannot bring in an answer, Frank, we can only open a way for life to go on."

To his Father, a businessman with a method for resolving problems and finding solutions, Frank now proposed a course of action which recognised no final goal, but simply set a course. It was far from Richard-Symons' formula of the least cost for the significant people, it was no more than a place to set out from. His father would purchase in Frank's name a dwelling which would allow him to be recognised as a property owner. He would live there with Nobomi as his domestic, this being the only legal way for her to be in a white area after curfew and run errands in such a part of town without harassment. Beyond this, there would be no plan, but Nobomi would have her child and could continue to live there for as long as she wished, because Frank would stay until she found a way to leave.

"That is preposterous, Frank. She might never leave. You would be giving up your life at her behest."

"I have a job. I will have a life. Perhaps not with the same prospects, as if I were back in England, perhaps not with the same opportunities for training and advancement, but it will be my life."

"The colonial underclass."

"No Father, the man of honour you educated me to be."

"You do not owe a debt of honour for your brother's indiscretions."

Frank knew those words could have been his own a year ago, but now they sounded ingenuous, even wanton. There were aspects of Harry that he had wished for in himself, that occasionally he had tried to copy (though his copying had been more like mimicking), but not all, and he wondered whether, were the tables turned, Harry would make a similar sacrifice. But he knew for himself that he would not go back on his word, and to Nobomi he had said, 'I will not leave you alone.'

"It is not just a debt of honour, Father, it is not even for the most part a debt of honour. Nobomi is trapped. It is a debt of humanity. I will do it because I can, with your help of course, Father. It will change my life, but I will never know whether it was for better or for worse. So it cannot matter."

After a pause: "Will you support me now? Please."

For all these lofty words and intentions, Frank still felt his actions were tainted. He was uncomfortable with the compromise he was being forced to make to satisfy the political reality that white people somehow had a higher status. The economic reality of unequal distribution between the racial groups was hard enough, but now the economic divisions seemed to be reinforcing an inhuman perception of difference as well. East London was already segregated in many respects. Was this all it could be, or could it get worse? But then he recalled Isabella's words, "we can only open a way for life to go on."

~~~

The deal was made, a path had been found. I would be giving way to wishful thinking if I thought there had been rejoicing at the outcome, but maybe Isabella noticed the glimmer of a smile on Nobomi's face as she watched and listened to Frank explaining what his father had agreed. A loving smile? No, they were not in love. Something more profound.

~~~

White Cat

Over the next few weeks, Frank took to making jottings, often on scraps of paper, as things occurred to him. We should probably think of them as a journal. I wished he had used a book of some form and then they might have survived as a primary account, instead of in the more random form of memories of various people who came into contact with them in different ways. Most seem to have been for Louie, but not in a personal way. I am sure he will have sent some to her, but she made no mention of them and does not seem to have passed them on to Barbara. Perhaps she gave them to their mother and that might account for their disappearance. I have pieced together a few from various sources, and transcribed them into a readable form.

...

I am truly relieved. I sat in the chair for a long while after Nobomi had gone to sleep, to sort out the jumble of my thoughts and feelings. I am used to a jumble of thoughts when I try to work something out and I have a logical way of dealing with that and arranging thoughts into ideas. But I am not used to this jumble of feelings. They don't always have words to represent them. I cannot arrange things that I am not able to express.

...

Nobomi seems more relaxed and her mood has lifted a lot since the end of August. She seems more comfortable with her position as domestic *than I am. Perhaps it helps her because it means that she can live with me without it being romance. But for me it was not romance. For me it is now oppression and I am the oppressor. No, I suppose that is too strong. Mother and Father have a maid and a domestic at home and they do not oppress them. Perhaps I am being too sensitive. <u>That</u> is not something people used to think of me!*

...

The Municipality are tightening up on Locations for non-whites, using the 1895 regulations. Our neighbours, all older, are not really talking to me, mostly glances and suspicious looks. They ignore Nobomi.

...

Louie, I could do with you here. I feel very isolated. Father is still here, though I think he wants to return. He is a rock. But he lives at the Beach Hotel and I cannot go there every day. I am becoming afraid for Nobomi's safety. I try not to leave her alone outside work hours. The atmosphere in the town has changed even over the last few weeks. The camp has closed finally, so the Boer families have left and it seems to have made the divisions between people more pronounced. Mainly British (now mostly English) and indigenous, so that means white and black. But then there are the Germans (they have their own area too) and the Asians and the Afrikaans. A few days ago I found out that a prominent member of the municipal council lives only a hundred yards down the road. With the camp closing I have lost Isabella, because she has had to go up to Kronstaadt, though she said she would come back for the baby's birth. So I wish you were here, sister, but then also I do not, because it is less and less a pleasing place to be.

...

I am ashamed and embarrassed and angry. Yesterday our neighbour came up to me in the road and said I was letting down my fellow citizens by allowing Nobomi to wear her ordinary clothes when she was just a domestic. He said she might be questioned by the authorities or even accosted in the streets, because it would be thought that she was breaking the regulations. I told him that our family in England employed a maid and a domestic and simply required that they dress neatly and with sobriety. I did not see why I should break with our family tradition because I was in East London. He did not answer, but looked hatefully at me and tossed his head back and strode away.

...

Dear Louie, Isabella arrived back in time for her to deliver the baby. A girl. She will be called Ngoxolo, which means Peace. It was a great relief to me for Isabella to be here, though it is said that African women can manage these things well themselves. But Isabella inspires confidence. Everything seems to be well. Father came the next day. It was only the second time he has been here. His mind has been very shaken by everything that he has had to learn anew since he first arrived. He was smiling for the new baby, I am sure of that, but I think he was also terribly upset because he realised he wanted to be her real grandfather and he knew that he would have to leave and never see her again, and worse still that he would never be able to bring her to Mother. I am going to try to have a photograph taken. We cannot go to a studio, but I have a friend who knows a photographer from the Dispatch who might come to the house with his equipment and do a photograph. My friend says he is one of the Germans and so does not so much mind tricking the Council, which is mostly English colonial.

…

We are on our own again. Nobomi has agreed to the photograph, but she needed me to persuade her when she realised that it would be made by another European. I cannot tell whether it is my imagination, but she seems to be going into herself again. I sometimes think it must be oppressive for her that she is surrounded by white society and language and our way of doing things. This is even though it was her own people who abused her when she arrived here two years ago. I wonder what it is like for her. I have told her I do not want her to dress as a domestic and I will take the risk and let them take me to court if they dare. I know that was foolhardy for me to say that, but I wanted her to know that to me she was as good as anyone. She told me I must not do that, not for me and not for her and Ngoxolo, because they would come for them as well. She said that she felt closer to me than to Harry in a special way. Between me and her romance did not get in the way and she knew that for me she was special just because of being who she was and she could see that I was only feeling at peace when she was feeling at peace as well. She called it ubuntu. She said it was the belief of all Bantu peoples.

...

Dear Louie, Father has left. He came yesterday to say goodbye to Nobomi and Ngoxolo and today I went with him to the dock. It will be a very different voyage for him going back. I think it will be good for him to be away from here, in the fresh sea air - for it can be very oppressive here on land, even with wind blowing in from the ocean. I hope the voyage will be a tonic for him. We both had difficulty holding back our tears. He must feel he has lost so much. Look after him well when he arrives home, as I know you will.

...

Nobomi talked about Father tonight. She said at first when we all met on the dock she had been scared and she expected him to ignore her. Then she realised that he was scared too. She saw that he was from a different world and he did not know anything that could help him understand what was happening to him. She said it was like that for her the night she was raped. It happened and she could not understand the world and what was happening to her. But she found Harry. And then me. "You were there for both of us, your father and me." She said, "Hug me Frank, just this once." As we hugged she said, "Remember, I am Mfengu." After that we went to our separate rooms.
...

Frank thought he had heard Ngoxolo crying in the night and so he was not surprised that Nobomi was not around when he got up. He made his breakfast and left for work, as had become the custom these mornings recently because of the feeding patterns of the baby. He noticed that he was a little restless during the day, not able to settle and concentrate in his usual way, and, though never one who watched for the clock to signal the time for closing, he realised that he glanced at it a few times during the afternoon. It was with some relief that he cleared away his materials at the end of the day, lifted his hat from the stand by the door, and left.

He caught the patch of white on brown in the corner of his eye as he turned from closing the door. The note was on the table...

"Dear Frank, you have been so good to me. I believe you know I cannot stay. Today maybe, tomorrow perhaps, but not always. So I go now. I will have Peace. Do not worry.

Thank you. Thank you.

Nobomi

~~~

Frank had never felt so alone. He was back in the desolation and the despair of the days when he was trying to understand he had lost his leg. The same incomprehension at losing a part of himself. The same world around that understood nothing.

He sat on the verandah most of that night. In the morning he bought an oil lamp and a large drum of oil and each evening as it got dark he lit the lamp and hung it on the verandah, so that every night it burnt… in memory?… in hope?… who can say?

He wrote to Isabella in case Nobomi had gone to her, though he did not believe she could have found her way that far. Isabella replied more than once that there had been no sign and she had not heard any news of her. She wished Frank good health and fortune along whatever course his life took him.

Eventually he wrote to his father and told him that he would wait a few more months in case Nobomi might still need somewhere safe to return to, but then he would sell the house and return home. He asked him to be understanding that he could not act more quickly.

He lived on in the house those months, as the regulations in East London became more and more restrictive for non-whites. No letter appeared. There was no report in the Dispatch. No call at the door. No word ever came.

In July 1905 Frank returned to England.

dark and light

Author's journal 13th December 2021

I found almost nothing that related to the first few years after Frank returned to England. I am sure he was severely shaken by his experience in South Africa - what had been intended as an adventure - today we might have called it a super gap year, only longer - had turned into almost continuous trauma. He was an emerging engineer, he had an engineer's way of thinking, each piece fitting perfectly into place, but for those 5 years of his life, almost nothing had fitted into place.

Don't we mostly live believing our notions of certainty? Thinking the script is there, written as we want it to play? As if our life is a stage set out as we want it to be?

I know that Frank took up a position as design engineer at a plant in the West Country making tyres. In the same firm there was a secretary with whom he fell in love and at 35 he married. This was Mollie (as she was known), the daughter of the Norwegian sea captain who gave Barbara her "slightly Scandinavian" looks. She became his devoted wife for the rather short time they were to have together. Soon after they were married, Frank took up a position as factory manager at a tyre and rubber company in Leyland and was provided with a company house, which Barbara later described to me as "really rather grand". He was living just the other side of the Pennines from where Isabella had attended school.

On 11th June 1917 Barbara was born.

In October the following year Richard-Symons died.

~~~

Frank was an innovator. The company made solid tyres, which were still the norm for a wide range of vehicles. His innovations included a new assembly method and an improved tyre profile, the two offering a more durable and comfortable ride at a lower price. And he had another asset for his employer - his wooden leg! In common with many manufacturers during and after WWI, the company was looking for ways to diversify, and started designing and making prosthetic legs, for which there was now a high demand. Because of Frank their designs were innovative.

He was a significant asset and he was highly regarded by the firm:

HBP/DH   May 15th, 1918

Mr. Cole,
Solid Tyre Development, Leyland

Dear Sir,

At a meeting of the Directors held May 6th, it was decided to increase your salary by £100 per annum. I think you are safe in assuming this to mean that the Directors are reasonably satisfied with the Solid Tyre Department, and after its many vicissitudes in the past, I think for once in my life I will say "Congratulations Cole."

Yours faithfully,

p.p. Wood-Milne Ltd.,

Sgd. p.p. H.B.POTTER,
DH

Sept., 1919 - Further advance, £50 per annum.

Feb., 1920 - Further advance, £14 per annum.

June 1920 - Bonus of £250 for manufacturing improvements.

This reward was in addition to a similar one made only four months previously following his confirmation as the most successful unit manager for the company.

And so the family was able to live comfortably and to Mollie and Frank were born three of their four children with Barbara the eldest. The First World War was over, and the chaos which followed that conflagration, took hold in continental Europe, while manufacturing Britain was able for a few years to continue its advancement into the industrial era. We might wonder where Frank would have been if the loss of his leg had not excluded him from any active service. He was not by nature a fighting man, but he was a patriot and he would have felt the call to that conflict very differently from that of the Imperial call to protect its colony.

But the economic tide turned and another innovation superseded Frank's new solid tyre and brought wider application of the pneumatic tyre. This time a different tenor to the director's letter:

HBP/DH　　　　　　　　30th March, 1921.

Mr. Cole,
Wood Milne Ltd., Leyland.

Dear Cole,

You know the condition of business at the present time. I have made every endeavour to try and place you, but without success, I am, therefore, reluctantly compelled to hand you a cheque for three months salary in lieu of notice.

I shall be always glad to answer any reference you may care to put up to me, and to state that it was only through absolute lack of business that we are obliged to let you go.

Yours sincerely,
Sgd. p.p. H.B.POTTER,
DH

Frank was adrift again, now with a family who depended on him. They moved south, to be within easier reach of his sisters, who supported him throughout the growing gloom and recession, during which he was never able to find employment worthy of his talents.

In 1930 he was diagnosed with cancer of the liver, from which he died. It took 5 weeks. He was 50.

Barbara was 13.

White Cat

Letter from Barbara to Louie 15th November 1930

Dear Auntie Louie,

I hope you do not mind me writing to you, but since the others have gone away to that boarding school Auntie Nora arranged for them, it has been very quiet here and I spend most of my time looking after Mother and she doesn't really talk to me. I probably should not say things like that but of all the relatives you are the one I thought would understand and wouldn't get me into trouble. It's not that I have anything big to say, just I miss Father and I suppose I am lonely. Everything feels empty now. Mother takes me up to stand by his grave almost every day. I don't understand why, because he is not there. And then I realise he is not anywhere, and I know very little about him. I only know about the last 13 years (well, most of them) and there was a lot more before I was born. I wish I could come and talk to you about him, because I have the feeling that you and he got on together specially well. I do not understand why no-one talks about him. I know that's not quite true. You talk about when you were all children and growing up, but then there is a big gap until he was up in

Leyland. What happened in between? Why won't anyone tell me? Do you remember that time when you three Aunties were here and all of you and Mother were in the sitting room talking with the door closed and I came in without thinking and everyone just went quiet? Mother looked as if she could have killed me (and she really told me off afterwards by the way) and Auntie Nora asked something like "Are you pleased not to have to go to school any more?" Why was she thinking that? And then there was the way Mother went round clearing up everything of Father's that was lying around, all sorts of little things, anything he used, and she cleared out his desk, including the drawer that was always locked, and she put everything in a big box and took it to hide in their room. She thought no-one saw what she was doing, but I saw. And then she got to the top of the stairs and the neighbour called in because the front door was open and she had to go down again before she could hide the box away. I had time to lift the lid of the box. I was looking for his pen. I wanted something that he held a lot. But as I found the pen I saw this photograph of a black girl holding a baby. It was like a postcard on the back but it had not been written on or posted, so I suppose someone gave it to him as a souvenir somewhere. Anyway, I have it now. I think it will be alright because I closed up the box very carefully, so I don't think Mother suspected anything. Promise you won't tell, please. I suppose I had better go because I have things to do now. This is an awful letter, it only has one paragraph. Whatever you do please do not let Auntie Nora see it, she would tell me off for my poor composition as well as what I have said. I trust you, Auntie Louie, and I hope you are keeping well, even though it is winter.

Love from,

Barbara

ps. I hope it will be alright if I write again

Letter from Louie to Barbara 20th November 1930

Dear Barbara,

It was lovely to hear from you, even though your letter was rather sad, and I will be pleased if you write again whenever you want to.

dark and light

I am sorry that it has been so difficult for you since your father died. And it makes me sad to hear how difficult his loss has been for your mother and this meaning that she is not able to help you as you are helping her. I will hope and I will pray that time gradually lightens the weight of her loss so that you and she are able to truly be mother and daughter for each other again.

It is very natural that when we lose a big part of our life, we become so very acutely aware of what we no longer have, and that includes what we do not know. I suppose that is because we realise that what we have of the person is all that we shall ever have. I know I am being a little abstruse and that is probably annoying for you. I think you are quite like me in many ways, and I don't like people being abstruse. You are right that your father and I were special for each other, but he could also be annoying. I often said to him, "You are not telling me everything", and he usually wasn't, but it didn't make any difference. I think he let himself off in his own mind, because he was a man. Men!!

But this is woman to woman and I need to ask you to trust me that I will not hide anything I don't have to hide, but Father, my Father, forbad all talk about some things. However, when you are of age I think I will be able to allow myself to tell you more.

You are very astute being curious about the "big gap" as you call it. A lot happened, including things which you could not possibly imagine or even guess. But one thing that you can be completely sure of is that your father was a good man and acted honestly and honourably through everything. Do not ever doubt that, my dear. Now that has not really given you what you want, but it is all I can do at the moment, and, well, you are closer than you think to your answer. Can that be enough for now?

With love,
from your Aunt Louie

~~~

<u>Letter from Barbara to Hugh 15th October 1948</u>

Dear Hugh,

He? She? is beautiful. Thank you for your very kind thought, though it has caused me some problems, as you might imagine. But I get the feeling that doesn't really bother you. You act when the moment comes and what comes after has to take care of itself. Like when you brought me back from Bath and you slashed the tyre of my bicycle. I still think about that, you know. I didn't even see it happen and I never really saw the knife before it was gone again. What was it? Some kind of commando knife? So you fascinate me, and you scare me, and that afternoon you got some way to seducing me. And <u>that</u> scares me.

So, no more presents. But, why a white cat?

Thank you though, and look after yourself, and keep safe,

<u>Barbara</u>

Letter from Hugh to Barbara 30th October 1948

Dear Barbara

Oh dear! Faux pas. I really did not mean to offend, but you are right, I just act, not quite without thinking, but the thinking has already happened when the action is in progress. Simultaneous you might say. I do think ahead as well, but not once the action is started.

Why a white cat? Well, I was always told that white cats mean happiness and prosperity and rebirth, and that seemed like a good thing to be wishing for anyone after what we have been through these last few years, and especially for someone who feels like quite a special person. (You.) That does not _have_ to mean any more than that you seem to be a person that helps the world along, not someone who is always looking for what they can get out of it. I think that's you. (The first type I mean, the type that helps the world along.) But you don't make a great show of it. And no-one would notice unless they happened to be there at the time. (I'm sure there's a lot you haven't told me.) That description reminds me of how my father talked about a Quaker nurse he worked with when he was conscripted and sent to Vienna after WW1 - no show, she was just there doing what needed to be done. And that's cats as well, they make no sound moving around, they just do what they are there to *do, and if a <u>white</u> cat crosses our path then we are truly fortunate.*

Till our paths cross next, so long white cat,

Hugh

~~~

Did it come back to her mind because she was reading this? Perhaps. Because she found she was crying and she wasn't sure why. (The girl's name had been Eva, but how did she know that?) Eight years ago now. It had been an evening like all the others - no show, she was just there, doing what needed to be done.

~~~

<u>Letter from Peter to Barbara 30th October 1948</u>

Dear Sis,

What's all the panic about? Are you more worried that this guy's going to take advantage, or that you're going to let him? And as to whether he is suspicious, well, perhaps I made too much of that stuff about Vienna and how dodgy it is. It's true you would expect an army officer to be in uniform when he was travelling, even off duty, if only so that he doesn't have to pay for anything. You could ask him what his unit is and what sort of stuff they are doing. But he sounds a regular fellow, probably had some advance training, so that's what he is - a soldier a long way away and you can keep him at a distance if you want to.

<u>Do</u> you want to? That's the real question.

I can't help much on the psychological stuff - women and babies and such like. As you can imagine, it's not really my world. But I do see it's a big thing for you. (And I do agree the child-producing pattern in our family has been a little strange.) You are normally quite ordered in the way you tackle things, so why not make a list of the things he would have to say (and you would have to believe) so that you decided to leave Norman and be with him? And then work out <u>what</u> questions you need answered, and <u>how</u> you need to ask them in order to get genuine answers. And also, - very important this bit - make sure you list everything that, if it came up, would rule him out regardless of anything else.

I think this means that I am going with your need to have children as being the most significant aspect of all this. But whatever you do decide to do, even nothing, I will be behind you, I promise.

This is your kid brother trying to be a bit less flippant than last time, I hope you realise that. I do have my more sober moments occasionally. I am aware we don't really know anything about our missing uncle, but sometimes I wonder if I might have his character traits. There do seem to be two fairly distinct types in the family. But we'll leave that for another time, when you've plumbed the Louie archive for more from her horde of secrets.

Please pass on my sincerest good wishes to everyone and especially my love to Mother and tell her I really will write soon because I have some things to send her. And keep smiling, for me as well,

loving good wishes,

Peter

~~~

Vienna in November 1948 was on a frontline. The Berlin blockade had just begun and the allies knew that a similar confrontation could arise in Vienna. These were the two cities where the Russians and the allies met, the cities similarly divided between the four powers, though in the case of Vienna the arrangements were even more complex. Each power had a sector of the city and in addition there was a central sector, run in turn by each country and with a joint command council. All investigations, arrests and questioning was performed by groups of four officers, but the motivations of each might be different according to their country's policy and pressures. Broadly one would say Russia and West, the West being driven by USA and Britain, but still there were 'nuances' beneath the ideological umbrellas. Russia was seeking to extract the maximum economic advantage from the occupation and create a vassal state from a partitioned Austria. The West was seeking a self-sufficient Austrian state, democratic and unaligned. Russia, in full occupation of the country for over a year before the partitioning between the four powers, had created a network of informants and sympathisers throughout government agencies, the police and the para-military in the city and used it to maintain a clandestine hold extending across all aspects of the city's life. Kidnappings and disappearances were frequent, interviews and investigations brutal, and not confined to their own sector.

dark and light

It was clear that Peter, through his connections, knew something of this. His attempt to play down his earlier rather alarmist description of the city may have worked, at least for a while, for Barbara, who still did not know Hugh's unit or location, or that Louie's suspicions about an officer of the occupying army travelling in civvies, was typically perceptive and astute. Had she not decided to follow a picturesque and somewhat circuitous route from Vienna to Salzburg, Louie and Hugh would never have met, because Hugh was en route to Graz, where the command of Field Security Section, the designation for British military intelligence in the field, was based in Austria. In fact he was on his way to his first briefing and special training following secondment from his own unit, the 138th Infantry Brigade.

Throughout 1948 the fears of the Western powers that Russia was in a position, and possibly preparing, to march over all agreed demarcation lines into western Europe, were growing steadily. That they would probably be able to achieve this more easily in Austria than anywhere else added further to the frenzy of espionage activity in Vienna, where every intelligence service had ears in each others' zones, where the political scene was extremely fluid and the communist party a high profile operator in that scene, where the police and their paramilitary wing were infiltrated by Russian operators, and where private spy-masters ran their own rings and passed information to the most 'profitable' outlet. Early in November an Austrian minister and a high-ranking official were arrested by the Russians as they were about to cross into the US sector. On behalf of the Americans they charged the official with fabricated allegations and sent her to the Gulags for 7 years. 'Favours' were exchanged amongst all the intelligence services as well as the private operators as seemed most efficacious at the time. In the middle of all this the reach of far right-wing groups was growing and a nazi party was gaining influence in the political scene, to the extent that it even won a significant minority of seats in the 1949 election.

Whether or not Hugh might have chosen to give Barbara even a sketchy picture of the true nature of the world into which his posting was about to take him, he would very soon be prevented from giving even the slightest hint. For significant periods he would not be able to risk any communication at all.

On his way back to Vienna from Graz he changed trains and went instead to Salzburg, from where he would post a carefully worded letter. He rightly calculated that a letter posted from Salzburg, already well on its way to becoming a tourist centre again and so offering a source of hotel stationery for a casual overnight visitor, would give some cover for the genuine (but incomplete) update he wanted to give Barbara. He may well have only narrowly missed another encounter with Louie at the hotel. As it was he had to feign a rush to collect luggage for his train when he collided with her on the station the next day - to the stunned amazement of both - though he was grateful for being spared lengthy awkwardness and dissimulation, since on this occasion they were travelling in opposite directions.

He had finally been able to relax into his seat on the train, realising that deception was not his strong suit and wondering how he had allowed himself to be seconded for the mission on which he was now embarked.

shadow-play

<u>Letter from Hugh to Barbara 10th November 1948</u>

Dear Barbara

Here's hoping all is well with you and that the white cat has found somewhere comfortable to curl up and sleep, because that is about all cats seem to do. I'm sure that's not what you do though and I trust that whatever projects you have got on are going well. I'm still hoping that you will tell me more about your family soon - do you have any interesting aunts or uncles? I've always wished I did but our family line seems to have been very compact, which I suppose is an odd way to think about it.

Anyway, I wasn't writing to harass you about giving up your well-guarded secrets. I needed to make you aware that I am being seconded from my unit to another one for a few months. It means I am going to be moving into the central sector in Vienna. I had already been stationed in the British sector

shadow-play

in the city, but I am now being re-assigned in the central sector, which is run in turn by each of the four occupying powers and has staff from all four of them operating there. In a way you might think it is a kind of privilege, being where it all happens, seeing the larger picture unfolding and all that, but in reality it is more like a cauldron in there and there is so much stewing in the pot that it's difficult to be sure of anything. I'm not saying this to alarm you, but to explain that because everything is so tightly controlled in the interests of security and not giving away secrets, my writing is going to become a bit haphazard. I will not always be able to answer any letters you send me and even when I do I might have to be very vague about what I tell you. Like now, for instance, I cannot tell you exactly what I will be doing. I am involved this way because about 6 months ago I made a connection with an officer outside our sector who was moved onto work our people were interested in. That's it. That's all I can say. One good thing about it is that because of the sort of meetings I am involved

in, I don't have to be in uniform all the time.
I say that is a good thing, but when it came to
it and I left off my uniform for the first time
it felt very strange, almost inappropriate,
like I was pretending or even hiding!
Normally you think of a uniform as
something you can hide <u>behind</u>, but now 'no-
uniform' feels like something I'm hiding
behind. And it's a very quiet place, the 'no-
uniform' place. If you are in uniform,
especially as an officer, there are always
people acknowledging you or looking at you
or saluting or waiting for you or in some
way being conscious of you, and that makes
you conscious of yourself because of all this
going on. Take off the uniform and that
doesn't happen, or nothing like as much, and
it is as if silence had suddenly descended. I
found it made me uneasy. I think I always
have been uneasy with silence, because it's one
of my traits that I always want to move
things along and I'll always make
conversation. Maybe that's why you and I got
started.

Of course the irony is that just when I would really value human interchange and the boost we get from simply having other people to talk to about ordinary things, it's not going to be there, or not very much. And just when I might really want to have someone I know and trust to simply listen without judgment and be a reliable support for me - that's you, by the way - I am not going to have that either. It doesn't mean I won't be able to write at all, but it is not going to be regular, or as often and, like I said, sometimes it will be guarded.

I need to ask you not to put any specific questions about what I am doing or what is happening here, when you write. My mail should not be checked, but I need to be very careful about the risk of written material being intercepted or 'lost', and that applies in both directions. Maybe as time goes on and I get a better feel for things, it will be possible to loosen up a little, but it is my duty right now to be very careful.

Please don't be alarmed. The world isn't ending, we just have to be patient until the sun comes out again.

But if you decide you want to keep your distance from all this and block me out of your mind so that you can concentrate on the world you have around you, I will understand that, I promise. If you write back and just say NO, then you will hear no more from me. I give you my word.

Take care of yourself,

Hugh

~~~

In fact Hugh was cautious and somewhat anodyne in terms of the picture he painted of his secondment but, though it was not his intention (and so he had downplayed the risks involved), the effect on Barbara was instant and arresting. Wrenched from the dreaminess of her rather vague image of Hugh's 'humanitarian' Occupation (when her Aunt Louie's intuition was not whispering in her ear, that is) she was thrown into uncertainty and confusion. She lurched from her guilt-ridden questioning of her present home and future into the stark unremitting reality which presents itself to every woman cut adrift by her man's surrender to his duty. And between the two was, well, a disconnect. If she had been entertaining in her mind a scenario where there could have been two parallel worlds, however fanciful that might have been - a revolving stage on which she somehow could step off onto whichever boards were downstage at that point in the play - such a possibility was now for certain unavailable. Both worlds were still there, but their stages were in different theatres completely.

She wrote back immediately, but all she could put on the paper was - *YES still YES, don't go* - and rushed out to get to the post office before it closed.

She knew to busy herself to allow tension in her body to subside and arriving back went straight out into the garden to pick up leaves and neaten the lawn, even though such activity in the gathering twilight was going to seem a little strange to Norman when he got home.

Better not to think, though. For now. Thinking leads to speculation and lack of knowledge leads to pessimism and fear. Her life would move on, somehow, even if, with this turn of events, it felt like it was in suspense.

~~~

Hugh returned to Vienna and to his new living quarters in a fourth floor 2-room apartment in Grashofgasse, between Stephansplatz and the river. The location, the aspect and the entrance were sufficiently un-noteworthy for his purposes and convenient for his brief, though quite a way distant from the HQ of British Field Security Section in the city, to which he had always been attached for line of command purposes.

In some parts the centre of Vienna still resembled Ozymandias' great desert monument where the wind-driven sand compromised the imperious toppled head, rubble heaps of proud palatine structures cascading over skeletal roads and passages. In other parts the narrow streets and allies, into which light seemed to leak inadvertently, looked untouched by the war, though in these another archaic and ominous atmosphere prevailed. Vienna, this city at a meeting point between east and west for centuries, taken and re-taken by opposing empires, prized by a succession of princes, chancellors, archdukes, counts - paper tigers all, in the lore of Time's relentless levelling - Ozymandias in the shadow-play.

St. Stephans cathedral still stood serene, surveying from on high the specs of humanity crossing and criss-crossing its flagged square. Out on the Ring, so long as you allowed war's detritus to blur to a random attempt at urban landscaping, the Opera House seemed only slightly marked, until you looked closer and noticed the telltale shadows of soot behind the loggia pillars. This, Hugh had originally thought was his focus, or rather, the intrigue which now surrounded the re-construction of its gutted interior. As a flagship project to raise spirits, it was thought by the Administrative Council to be the ideal choice: Vienna had basked in its musical heritage for more than 200 years - the city of Beethoven and Schubert and Mahler - so that even those citizens who had no interest in music were aware of its undisputed standing. They dropped coins into the boxes which the council had put out around the streets in order that each citizen could feel they had contributed to the revival of this most iconic symbol of their heritage and the stature of their city.

But such an icon also had political value, and in Vienna, wherever there were political totems, there were always personal, party, national and political interests intertwined. Such was his world from now.

It was the next day when, weaving his way through the alleys of the old city from his lodging in Grashofgasse, passages seemingly in a time-warp, wondering if he would ever become familiar with such a labyrinth, he came abruptly into the looming presence of St Stephans cathedral. Despite its massive size and towering height it took him by surprise in the way that such edifices often do, their bulk somehow concealed by a cluster of the lesser structures they dwarf. But there it was, another of Hitler's trophies, the Dom he had driven around 10 years before in his symbolic gesture of subjugation of the city which *could* have rewarded instead his *peaceful* art, and saved the world the pogrom he unleashed... if it had only known. They serve no purpose, such musings, Hugh thought, and yet, when confronted with such wholesale and pointless destruction, cannot meagre man be forgiven for seeking the consolation of reflecting how near it had come to lighting on the civilised way? how, almost, it might not have needed the roll of the dice? and that next time... next time... so that this cannot happen again...

The heaps of rubble had mostly been cleared from the periphery of the open side of the cathedral precinct, which he was crossing. But the other effects of the bombardment, the burnt out interiors, the yawning window spaces, the ravaged supports of this or that notice board or street light or road-sign, all these were still in evidence. It seemed there was a hierarchy to the restoration process, he reflected, and somehow the icons must come first, doubtless for the contribution they could make to personal or party prestige; symbols also of the promises of Peace and Recovery and even, yes perhaps, Humanity. On this particular dreary half-lit morning these seemed like distant dreams, as minuscule as the figures of the children playing in the cathedral square, moving shadows cast against Stephans' brooding mass, their dwarf-like bustle a foil for its stillness.

He had not noticed the solitary figure at first, its slenderness merging into the church's architecture. Standing apart from the other children - she might have been 14, no more, he thought - not part of any group, apart *and* not part, he realised as he looked around, for she was not European, or not wholly anyway, dark-skinned, so that for a moment his mind glimpsed a native child looking wondrously across some vast and undefiled African plane. She turned and looked towards him and his instinct was to approach her, but then he realised he was not in uniform, so lacked the only possible symbol of trustworthiness in this murky world. He would not dare to even take her to one of the shelters without proof of authority. But then why *this* child anyway? There were thousands, tens of thousands even, in the city like this and somehow they survived, the ones that didn't die of dysentery or starvation. Besides, though probably living rough, she showed no obvious sign of that. His military mindset was regaining control now, but before turning away, he smiled. Whether she noticed, he could not tell, for even looking towards him her eyes still seemed to be fixed on an invisible far horizon.

As he came around the end of the Dom, past its ancient nave door, he looked back. She was still there, alone, a graceful forlorn figure, who surely didn't belong in this place.

~~~

"You must trust no-one except those who are your contacts in here," Major Roberts was briefing, "because the Russians have infiltrated everywhere. As you know they were in full occupation for almost a year before the zones were agreed, so they were in full control of our zone before we got here. You must assume that they have watchers, informants and sleepers everywhere, police, militias, government offices, party hierarchy, as well as out on the street. Cooperation is notional with the Soviets in the central zone, and there are even different agendas between the allies sometimes as well. You must never have any identification on your person other than the ID we will provide you with. You must memorise all telephone numbers you need. In your rooms leave around some things relating to your cover, but you must keep anything connected with your true identity hidden at all times - find the best place, ceiling, floorboards, whatever, and leave your own traces so that you can tell whether your hiding places have been compromised. Likewise when you go out, always leave a trace to warn you of intrusion. If you think you've been compromised, stay clear, do not come here, but contact us and wait for instructions." He paused. Military bearing prevented any overt indication of unease, but there was something, Hugh thought.

"I know you know all this. It must become second nature, though. We don't have time, but you will have to take time to embed. For the next 2 weeks do nothing except act your cover. Go to the obvious places, as well as the less obvious ones. Talk to ordinary people, personal stories, that sort of stuff. You might get a good book written, who knows?

"You know we're worried about Russian intentions with the elections coming up. If the communist party wins and the Soviets come over, we are not defending our position here, small holding operation, that's all. But make no mistake, they will walk it. The line is northern Italy and the eastern boundary of the French Zone.

"In that event we will call you with a code - the corporal will give you that. Get out west or south any way you can, but you will be on your own.

"Questions?"

"No Sir"

"Good luck. Dismissed."

Hugh acquainted himself with the necessary protocols, perused the daily bulletin for his level of clearance and left. He was heading back to Grashofgasse, but first gave himself a tour of key locations, the Opera, the Town Hall, the main crossing points to the Soviet sector, Karlsplatz and the Danube bridges. Finally he was back in his rooms and set about refining his security precautions.

He was the only occupier on the top floor, the roof level of the building, and so there were no other entrances from his landing. The stairs, typically for these buildings, wound round a narrow well in a rectangular formation coming to a landing every second turn. Being fairly certain there was no-one else in the vicinity, he went down a flight and examined the stair treads to find one that he could prise up and twist a little so that when replaced it did not exactly fit and would make a screeching noise against the adjoining support when trodden on. (He would remember not to use this stair himself except to check on returning.) Back in his room he found the rear of the bed's headboard had a panel which he could lift away and then offered a hiding place for papers and when replaced could be secured from the other side. Finally he found that the panel to which a portion of the window was attached for ventilation could be removed, leaving ample storage behind. It could be accessed by freeing the window, which could then only be put back in position with a different placement of the cord which held it.

Now satisfied with his precautions, Hugh descended into the outside world and walked up Kärntner Strasse to find a café where he could sit towards the rear of the salon, a position which afforded a view of the street through the classic broad windows, as well as of most of the other patrons. He was here certainly to watch, but also to practice the peripheral viewing he had been taught at Graz. It will need practice, a lot of practice, he was told, so take every opportunity you can. You are holding a conversation, or you are reading or working with something, and you focus your attention on the object or person involved. As you are doing this and without shifting your gaze, you turn your *mind* to observe what is in your peripheral vision. Find something of interest and without stopping what you were doing, watch whatever is there in your peripheral vision and in particular watch for any change or movement. Then go somewhere else out of your direct vision, but only in what your *mind* is looking at, your eyes must not shift at all: a person sitting in front of you and looking at your face must not see any change.

This is what Hugh spent the next half-hour practising as he perused his newspaper in the café on Kärntner Strasse. After this he headed back towards his rooms, but he stopped at a small café in Ballgasse. He sat at the back, took out his notebook and started a letter to Barbara.

~~~

Letter from Hugh to Barbara 12th December 1948

Dear Barbara

I'm here like I said I would be, in a little café in the old part of Vienna. I got your note, not sure how. You must have been in a rush. Almost in a panic. No need to panic, honestly.

I have settled in, but my accommodation leaves a little to be desired. I have two rooms, one with sink, etc. on the fourth floor (which is really the attic) in one of the of the eighteenth century terrace blocks which are everywhere in old Vienna. Working conditions are not ideal - one single bar electric fire and that's it. So it's cold, sometimes very cold and I have to put my heavy overcoat on. I don't like writing when I'm all clobbered up like that. And as for the nights - there's no question of undressing to get into bed! You'd think the Times of all the newspapers would want to put their people in reasonable accommodation for better productivity and all that - you can't write legibly with gloves on.

The good thing is that I'm right in the middle of the city and there are loads of cafés and bars and meeting places to hand. I need to find a few like-minded souls to get the feel of things here, so I'm going to join a music society and a literary group - contacts are all important and the paper wants my first piece next week! But I'm going to keep it on a social observation level, away from the political until I get a better feel for what is going on.

Social observation can be done anywhere, but then you have to make contact and talk to people. That isn't so easy because people here are reticent, even suspicious of strangers after what they have been through. So I will have to sit around cafés and squares and become one of the 'habitués'. That all takes time.

Children and how they've come through are likely to be my first topic. I am sure they are the most approachable group. I was walking across Stephansplatz this morning towards the cathedral and there was a group of children playing a running and chasing game right alongside the church - like tiny toys up against this enormous building. They were making quite a noise and there were some older people looking amused and others looking very reproachful and there was a rather grand looking lady who had just been collided with by one of lads... just the sort of word-picture a writer looks for to start a piece like this. I was completely distracted by all their commotion, but then I noticed that there was a young girl standing on her own away from all their mêlée and she was just standing completely still, looking into the distance. And it was like she didn't belong. For one thing she wasn't European, I thought she was probably African. And she was so completely self-contained. She looked at me, but her expression did not change and it was as if I was just part of the landscape. I had to get going but she took no notice and she never moved a step. I will admit I was a bit concerned, a young girl on her own who looked as if she was living rough - postwar Vienna is not a cosy place. There must be refuges for children, so I am going to make enquiries and now that my new Press Card *has come through just this morning, I am 'respectable' again and so I might be able to get her or any like her to a refuge and even keep up contact for an ongoing feature.*

So that's it. A story or stories in the making. Not much more I can say right now, but I will write again next week.

Keep your spirits up - there will be a future.

Fondest good wishes,

Hugh

~~~

It hardly needs to be said that there was almost nothing in the letter which made any sense to Barbara. It meant that he was not going to stop writing and that was a relief. And she was fascinated by his word-picture of the children in front of the cathedral. She smiled as she watched them in her mind but she wished there did not always seem to be a shadow following the happy scenes. And why did she feel unsteady just then? Something disorientating. Something out of place. Her mind was floating... a young girl appeared, but not the one Hugh described, because this girl was white. Somehow the same backdrop of destruction, piles of rubble, gutted buildings, and the girl was looking at her across the chaos. Her name was Eva, but how did she know that?

And then a low rumbling began, which became a thunderous crash, and she was gone.

Barbara shuddered. She looked out at her garden, and longed for the company of her infuriatingly imperturbable brother.

~~~

Hugh's cover was intended to give him multiple possibilities for contact. He was the Times reporter covering the social aftermath of the War in Austria and the attempts of the Allies to enable, through their occupation, the humanitarian re-construction of the country, officially a victim and not a defeated enemy. Hence the interest he could take in the ways the government was seeking to revive morale amongst the citizens with public works and projects such as the re-building of the Staatsoper. This in turn gave him plausible access, not just to much of the city's bureaucratic machinery, but also to other interested parties and their manoeuvring. Principal among these, and of most interest to the Allied military, was the Austrian Communist Party, who, with an election approaching towards the end of 1949 that would not bring them to power simply through the ballot box, were thought to be starting to stir trouble beneath a mask of benevolence and were even thought to be setting up an alliance for civil unrest with the half million disaffected nazis legitimately at large within the community. If extreme left and extreme right could find common cause in violence and community unrest, it could conveniently open up a path for a Soviet takeover of the whole country.

The first contact which Hugh made with 'the other side' came through the music society, the Wiener Musikverein, where he had fallen into conversation with Fritz Keller, a name he recalled had been mentioned to him by the acquaintance he made while with the 138th in Styria and which had ultimately led to his current secondment. Over drinks after a talk in the Burgtheater, Keller hoped that he would be able to mention in one of his pieces in the Times how the contribution of the communist party in terms of facilitating the smooth operation of the various construction works involved (which had in fact started and stopped several times), as well as their good offices with the Soviets to obtain financial assistance, were of critical importance. Rallying the Austrian people behind the project itself and the Austrian State Treaty, was important in all their calculations and uppermost, he knew, in the thinking of the Soviets and the Allies as well. "The Soviet Union and the Russian people," he continued, "with their great cultural heritage will be on the front line supporting the Austrian state in restoring the true artistic prowess of this great city after the ravages of the philistine Nazis."

"If you were able to clarify our part in this respect, there are others, associates of mine within our ranks, I could introduce to you who are also anxious to be understood and could in their own way present a picture I feel sure would interest your readers."

As he walked back to Grashofgasse that evening, Hugh passed through streets where rubble was still being cleared. A gang of ragged Nazi women were engaged in lifting dismembered sections of mortar and stonework and shovelling debris into barely-adequate handcarts, which others then trundled away donkey-fashion for filling craters. Groups of gratified citizens looked on - with relief or satisfaction? - and he was reminded of a photograph in a German newspaper acquired by his unit during the War, showing respectable Berliners strolling through their city's Zoo Garten, spectators for Gestapo guards leading naked Jewish men through the park... crawling. The coin had flipped, certainly, but with a sinister innuendo.

He was nearly back and strolling wistfully across Stephansplatz, but the square was empty... no homeward hurrying, no children chasing, no dark-skinned girl standing.

~~~

It was only a matter of a few days before one of Keller's 'associates' turned up at the café Hugh had told him was a regular haunt - had they been watching him in that time? If so he had not noticed. He introduced himself as Jürgen (no second name) and asked if he could re-fill his coffee.

"Fritz told me that you were interested in giving a balanced picture for Times readers of the political situation in Austria. That is of particular interest to us in the KPÖ[2], because we feel that British and American people especially are led to believe that we must be a threat to a stable Austria just because we call ourselves communists. It seems that your people unjustly believe that comrade Stalin, our great Soviet leader, is a man to be feared by your countries, though of course this is not true. But then you do not see how the Austrian Council manipulate public sympathy and misuse funds which should be re-building our honourable nation."

"I am a journalist," Hugh replied, "and so my first interest is reporting. I do not take sides, but instead my aim is to see that all sides are accurately and justly reported."

"That is all we ask, my friend. We want no more than this." He paused as if mentally scanning a check list, then, "I would like you to hear the honest concerns of our comrades for yourself. Our chairman sent me to speak to you first, but he would like to meet you himself. We are arranging a meeting of our committee next week and our chairman thought you might be interested in joining us. The day is not yet decided, but I could meet you on Tuesday in the café outside the park in Rudolfsplatz. It is a very pleasant place, a favourite of mine, and I will be able to tell you of the arrangements then. Would 6 be convenient for you?"

Hugh agreed. Jürgen smiled, promptly rose and left the café with only a brief farewell, a little as if he had

---

[2] Kommunistische Partei Österreichs, the Austrian Communist Party

completed his mission and was now dismissed, Hugh thought.

He had the luxury of a few days and so he left it until Friday before he reported the developments to the Major in order not to risk being seen near FSS[3] HQ when it was most likely that there would be watchers. When he did go he took time to saunter in the Stadtpark overtly people-watching before making his way over to Sebastianplatz to enter from a rear door. At the same time as filing a report on his recent meetings he submitted the copy for his first article which was to appear in Tuesday's Times under the title "Survivors Great and Small" with his cover byline - Hugh Winters. (He was relieved, of course, to know that his own text would be re-written by a competent ghost-writer.)

The following Tuesday, when he arrived at the cafe on Rudolfplatz, he saw from a distance that Jürgen was already there but standing outside. He had no time, however, to work through possibilities and options in his head for Jürgen saw him immediately and beckoned to him…

"My friend," he said, "I am sorry, but a small change of plan, for the meeting is tonight and our chairman has sent me with a car to collect you and take you straight there now. Please, here is the car, we will go now and when it is over, we will drive you back to your rooms." He indicated the Citroen at the kerb, opened the door

---

[3] Field Security Section were part of British Military Intelligence and drew personnel from all operational units

and ushered him inside, almost in one movement. Briefly Hugh wished for the shared understanding and protocol which had gone with a uniform, but he banished the thought quickly enough to be able to show his pleasant surprise at the consideration of his hosts.

The car came out onto Salztorgasse and took the direction for the Salztorbrücke. In less than a minute they were crossing the Danube into the Soviet sector. He realised immediately that comrade Jürgen had chosen their meeting place in order to have the minimum distance to cross over into the Russian-controlled part of the city. His sense of unease increased when he realised that their vehicle was recognised and acknowledged as they were waved past the Russian post on the bridge. If any part of the city could be considered safe for Allied military operating undercover, it was for certain not east of the Danube.

They stopped outside a building which looked as if it had been a warehouse and was part derelict and Hugh was invited to precede his escort up the steps to the main door, down a long wide passage and into a remarkably well-lit (for these times) room with a long table and four formally-attired middle-aged men sitting, poring over what looked like pamphlets. One of these rose to meet him: "Good evening Mr Winters, I am so pleased to meet you after this while and hope that this might be the beginning of a long and fruitful association. I am Johann Koplenig."

"I am honoured Herr Koplenig. I had no idea I was to meet a former Vice-Chancellor of Austria tonight."

"The honour is equally ours Mr Winters, for to have a reputed journalist from an influential newspaper like The Times is of great importance to us. Forgive me that I am not going to stay to your meeting, because I have Council business, but it was very important to me to meet you. And I hoped you would be able to tell me, I would like to read some of your recent work for the Times. Is there somewhere I can find something?"

"My first piece from Vienna is published today. It is called 'Survivors Great and Small'. I suppose today's edition will arrive here on Thursday."

"That's good. Thank you. Now if you will excuse me."

As Koplenig departed, Hugh was motioned to sit on one side of the table and found himself on his own facing the three men left in the room. There were no more introductions.

The evening was beginning to feel choreographed and their meeting beginning to appear scripted. Their focus appeared to be the elections in the next year and being able to position themselves visibly as the nation's, that is the people's, protector against corruption and manipulation by the other political parties. They were already working for the nation by helping to smooth out misunderstandings which threatened the steady progress with re-building, they were supporting the improvement of housing standards and were fighting hard for new housing projects across the city. (This, it was pointed out, was of course easier in the east of the city than the west, where personal interest and profit were always present.) Finally their contribution to the artistic re-birth of the city could not be denied - the new Staatsoper would be a beacon to banish the grey misery of postwar Europe.

And then he was dismissed. His departure was as unexceptional as his arrival. The same driver was waiting to take him back across the river, this time without Jürgen who had excused himself to work further with his comrades. This came as something of a relief for Hugh who did not want to lead anyone into the proximity of Grashofgasse. The driver accepted without question his request to deposit him near the Burgtheater, though he still took the precaution of walking in a circle away from where he needed to go. He finally arrived at his rooms very tired and discomfited, though he could congratulate himself that his emotional disturbance did not distract him from checking his security devices before anything else.

~~~

Letter from Hugh to Barbara 22nd December 1948 (early hours)

Dear Barbara

I think I should attempt some clarification, since my last letter must have been very puzzling for you. I am afraid it was necessary for me to send something to you in order to establish where I was and get a feel for a new work routine - really as much in my own mind as trying to pass on information.

What I can tell you is that it is more difficult than I expected living on my own. I have two rooms and once I am up here it is like there is no other person in the world. No view except roofs and only the odd sounds from somewhere else in the building. It is almost as if there is no-one else living in the block, though I cannot believe that is the case given the housing shortage in the city.

Vienna is very quiet in the evenings. The cafés, where I spend a lot of my daytimes writing, close quite early. I have now joined a music society and a literary society to get some connections, which helps. There is a lot about this city which is quite unnerving and I suppose I feel a little unprotected. I think you know what I mean. I look just like any other person in the street.

Tonight I have been out late to a special meeting connected with the music society and I got a bit lost getting back, so it is now the early hours and perhaps I had better think about bed. I hope I sleep in tomorrow. Of course the white cat would be good company.

Take care of yourself, dear Barbara,

Hugh

ps. Happy Christmas!! but I think it will be too late by the time you get this.

<u>Letter from Barbara to Hugh 30th December 1948</u>

Dear Hugh

Thank you for your letter which helps a little.

It was a difficult Christmas, but not as difficult as yours I am sure. I spent most of it thinking about you and wondering what is really going on for you. I am not sure whether it helped or not, but a while ago Peter gave me some hints about what might be happening. He was in the army in India during the War and he still has a friend who was posted to Vienna a couple of years ago. I think he has left now. But I have an idea... and it scares me.

I think it scares me, not just for you, but also for me. What does that mean? Do you realise? All the way back from Bath that Saturday evening I was trying to work out a way I could make you miss your train. I came up with all sorts of mad ideas.

Why am I talking like this? I think it's because it is getting more difficult. At home I mean. If I tell you, you must not find a way to feel guilty about it, because it pre-dates you by quite a bit. In short it isn't working, Norman and me. And that's because of me. Wrong expectations. We got married in 1942, the year after the worst of the blitz. Panicking to live while we could, I suppose. In my defence - what I could not know was how desperate I would be to have children. We decided it would not be right until the War was over... and then we found we couldn't, or we didn't. And no-one can tell us why.

And now, it's not that I am going to leave <u>because</u> we haven't had children - I presume that could be me - but, that is just another thing, and it is the biggest thing.

So when you get released and find your way back to these shores - though you haven't said you will come back, I know - I shall have bought a little caravan in a secluded park - I like Cleeve Hill in Frenchay - and be curled up with a cat. And I shall call it... I don't know what I shall call it, but I will try to find a white one. Or perhaps one will find me.

So, nothing to do with you, you see. Well, not much.

Please take care, you are precious to me,

Barbara

Letter from Hugh to Barbara 6th January 1949

Dear Barbara

I am writing straight back. Thank you for your confidences (and confidence). Your words are so touching and the sentiments which you express confirm the very best that I have ever believed about you. It must have been so difficult to write such things and to think that you have trusted me to hear such a heartfelt message...

There is nothing more that I can tell you at this moment, but I will write again very shortly.

Dearest Barbara, take care of yourself,

Hugh

~~~

A couple of days later Hugh took his latest Times article submission into FSS HQ. He needed the censors to vet it before it was transmitted to the newspaper for his ghost-writer to re-draft. His over-arching message was the necessity for collaboration (which had been lacking in the National Council since Herr Koplenig had ceded his position as Vice-Chancellor), but he had framed his argument with the implication that honest efforts at national consensus and cooperation were being thwarted at the level of the National Council.

His submission was passed by the censor without alteration and the following day he received notification that this article would be published the following Tuesday.

Two days after its publication Jürgen found him drinking coffee late in the afternoon at another café, one of his regular haunts but not where they had ever met before. Hugh wondered how he knew where to look for him. Was he being followed? If he was he had failed to pick it up.

"Our chairman, Herr Koplenig, has read your latest article and would very much like to show his appreciation in person. He was hoping that we could all meet again this evening. This evening he will have more time and would like to be more hospitable and informal. He suggests that I collect you again in the same way... or, I could collect you at your rooms, more appropriate, he said, for an honoured guest."

"I would certainly be pleased to accept," Hugh replied, "but it will be quite ok to meet you in the same way in Rudolfplatz, because I have a brief call to make quite close to there at the end of the afternoon."

As Jürgen left him, he felt again that relief at having avoided leading anyone to his rooms. But the relief was short-lived: on returning to Grashofgasse, he heard no sound as he stepped (as he always did as a check) on his dislodged stair tread. It took him by surprise. He moved cautiously to his door, and found it double-locked, as he had left it. Once inside, he surveyed the whole room from the door and then walked slowly all around both rooms without touching anything. Nothing amiss, he was thinking, until he saw that his silver pencil was resting the wrong way on his notebook on the table - the lead was pointing away, when, for as long as he could recall he had always placed it with the lead towards - he knew how it felt in his hand as he put it down.

He shuddered. No longer out of reach.

~~~

He was driven to a different location across the Danube that evening, and found himself in the faded reception suite on the third floor of a grand city mansion, some way beyond the canal, he thought. This time it felt more like a genuine gathering than a caucus. Herr Koplenig was in the middle of the room talking earnestly to a small group but broke off as soon as he was ushered in, welcomed and thanked him effusively for coming and guided him across to the group he had just left. Jürgen had already slipped away.

"This is really a gathering of friends, Mr Winters, and I wanted to take the opportunity to introduce you, of course, but also to show you that we are a group of ordinary citizens who want the best for all the people of our country."

The company was dressed quite formally, but had an air of a social gathering, and there was a significant amount of wine and liquor on the table at the side of the room.

"First I must make a very important introduction," continued Koplenig, "because quite unexpectedly this evening we have a visit from Comrade Aleksey Petrov, who is on the personal staff of Commandant Dimitry Abakumov." (Hugh knew that Abakumov was the new overall military chief of the Austrian Russian sector.)

Introductions courtesies formalities flatteries, the stuff of *faux* friendship and bonhomie, he well knew.

The party gradually coalesced into meeting formation with a top table of six, of which he was one and, Hugh now saw, Fritz Keller (his original contact at the

Musikverein) another. Facing them the grave looks of around twenty listeners.

Koplenig began: "Comrades, our special meeting tonight is to welcome Aleksey Petrov representing the new commandant of the Russian sector. We would like him to see that our hopes for the Austrian people are in line with Soviet aims in our country and in harmony with the vision of comrade Stalin. We also have with us Hugh Winters, the respected reporter from the Times newspaper in London, who will be based in Vienna for a few months to post despatches to his newspaper which genuinely reflect what is most important for our people. He is known to be honest and insightful in his writing and his newspaper is renowned for its unbiased commentary on world events. I hope he will address us a little later, but first comrade Keller will open with some thoughts on our strategy in the build-up to the election in October."

Keller seemed to Hugh to be from the stern unsmiling mould of Marxist party official, now that he saw him away from the relaxed setting of the music society. His clipped exhortations to the group before him came from the cold unforgiving directive style of the Party handbook. The election being 8 months away there would be no let-up in the twin thrusts of their public propaganda and their covert cultivation of strategic connections and alliances. The former, cloaked in patriotic sentiment and expressions of universal goodwill, would be their public image and would, he was sure, be echoed in the writings of their now ally in the world of influential international media (and he looked across to Hugh as he said this); the latter would ensure that, where the interests of the Party and the movement required, they would have the channels available to set in place the levers of influence. "I mean, of course, that we will not pass up any opportunity to ensure that respected and faithful colleagues and comrades are present in all police, militia, paramilitary and defence units which are essential to the efficient and beneficial functioning of any well-ordered society." He went on: "Furthermore, we must keep in mind that even the ideologically opposite can combine in a common cause, when it is the means of execution which *is* the cause."

Hugh presumed that what he was hearing was a starting signal for all the caucuses represented in the room for action which each individually had in readiness. In his own address to the meeting he sought to play on this to tease out more detail. He wanted to be able to make clear their laudable aims, which would certainly find sympathy among readers of his newspaper, but he also wanted to ensure that he did not inadvertently allude to any aspects of their activities which could be misinterpreted or judged adversely. To which end he hoped that they would keep him informed of anything of this nature in order that he could ensure that their message to the world would not be misunderstood or compromised.

Comrade Petrov, in whose unremitting gaze he seemed to have been permanently fixed, declined to address the meeting, and after some anodyne and repetitive contributions from the floor it was left to Koplenig to conclude the business. The gathering then broke into smaller groups of earnest discussion and equally earnest drinking. It seemed to Hugh that he was being steered on a course between groups which were briefed with material for his consumption. Of more interest for him were the occasional words which he could discern with an auditory version of the peripheral viewing he had been practising. Words like 'cell' and 'industrial' and 'community' and 'nazi'.

The assembly was late to disperse, causing Hugh considerable anxiety about his accompanied return over the river. Whilst he might have allowed that 'they' knew where he lived now anyway, he was well aware that there were multiple factions and interests in all circles in the city and his driver that night could have a different allegiance from the intruder. He opted to be put down in Kärntner Strasse near Neuer Markt on the pretext of needing to phone his office to check the printing for his next submission, this being just possible with the time difference to London. He followed through with the call and then took a tortuous route through pedestrian allies, parks and subways back to Grashofgasse.

It was not until he was finally back in his rooms, having checked his security devices, that he felt the tension, which had been rising steadily during the evening, finally start to subside. Relief at last. And no further intrusion.

~~~

Letter from Barbara to Hugh 4th March 1949

Dear Hugh

It seems too long since I wrote. That's not because I am not thinking about you. I am. Practically constantly. So constantly that Mother has started to notice when I go and visit her (she lives quite close you see). She doesn't like you not listening to her when she is talking, so she watches for telltale signs. She has these rather sarcastic ways of getting your attention. So, in the middle of telling you about her trip to the grocer that morning, in the middle of a sentence even, when you're gazing out of the window she'll say, "Oh I hadn't noticed they had pulled that house down opposite," or, "Will you be long counting the pigeons, dear?" or, "Peter said he's getting married." Well that one would certainly get us listening, but never mind why, that's for another day. Mothers!!

Apart from my being obsessed with what's happening to *you*, I think it's also you *and* Vienna. The idea of Vienna has started to fascinate me, but not entirely in a good way. My Aunt Louie has started to go to the

Salzburg festival again (she went every year before the war), and this year she made a detour and went via Vienna. She's a funny old bat, but lovely, never got married, three sisters and none got married, theirs was the generation that ran out of men after the First War. Archetypal English Gentlelady, that's Aunt Louie. She's into family history, knows lots of tidbits going back several generations, some she's told me, some she won't. Probably thinks I'm not old enough. But she did tell me about an uncle that all through my childhood and teens I never knew even existed! That was a shock because she sent me his burial certificate - in East London, which is in South Africa! His name was Harry and he had a girl-friend who was having a baby. It had something to do with my father too. But isn't it strange? You get a connection with something or somewhere that hadn't featured in your life at all up to that point, and then it starts appearing everywhere and seems to connect all over the place. Like you and your father being in Vienna. Oh, and that's what I wanted to ask you - do you remember the name of the Quaker nurse he worked with? Aunt Louie again - some old family connection.

I'm woffling. I hope it's not too boring. I really want to talk about when you get home and you can start your new life here, but that doesn't seem quite appropriate somehow.

Peter wrote to me and gave me a local story (local Gujarat India, that is) about a white cat. I'll tell you sometime. I'm making a list of all the things I am going to tell you that do not seem to lend themselves to sending in a letter. Sometimes you need to see the other person's reaction as you tell them something, which of course means you change slightly how you are telling it, but then it becomes something shared. That's my feeling anyway.

I think I must go, I am getting a bit emotional.

Come back soon,

Your dearest Barbara

~~~

To Hugh's surprise, he heard nothing more from Jürgen or Fritz Keller for more than 2 weeks. While he had to assume that his whereabouts was known to at least one element in the communist party and so he was open to being approached, he himself had no way of initiating contact with any of those he had met on his evening excursions. The only exception was Herr Keller who was also a member of the Musikverein, which Hugh continued to attend regularly, though Keller did not appear. He could not tell whether his hint that he be given information on the pretext that he would be able to pre-empt any bad press, had been premature. He sought to widen his catchment: whilst diligently maintaining the times and locations he had established as routine, he added others in different districts around the old town and focused more actively on the Austrian Literature Society based in an old city mansion on Herrengasse in the vicinity of the Burgtheater and the town hall. But the next contact, when it came, followed a similar pattern to the previous ones, though the link was no longer Jürgen, who appeared to have been replaced by a Gunther. The location for the meeting was different as well, much further beyond the Danube, in what appeared to be a private house beyond the outskirts of the city and, as far as Hugh could tell, some way towards the Hungarian border. He was shown into a room with Herr Koplenig and Fritz Keller. There was no-one else.

Keller began: "Mr Winters, we have asked you to join us this evening to discuss with us a matter of great importance in the coming months and to be privy to our great concerns about the future of our country. Herr Koplenig believes that we should trust you to hear without bias or prejudice these concerns and relate them with honesty and appropriate emphasis to ensure that our position in the people's perception will allow us to influence justly the course of events."

Koplenig was more precise: "You will be aware, Mr Winters, that our party, and myself as Vice-Chancellor, were forced from the governing coalition some months ago. This move was unconstitutional and based on false allegations and a series of misunderstandings. It is now of the greatest urgency that we redress this by all means at our disposal in view of the elections which are to take place for the Governing Council in October this year. You will realise that it is vitally important that our party is represented at the highest level as we approach the final stages of preparation for our country's independence through the Treaty."

Hugh's interest may have been sparked by what he heard as a barely concealed invitation to partisan commentary on unfolding events and their unexceptionable anticipation, but he knew that he must maintain his pretence of genuine commentary alongside an openness to being influenced by his hosts' arguments. And so: "I am sympathetic to your outline of your country's situation and all the points you are making about your party's need to be understood in the country, but I am not sure what it is that you believe I can do in this regard. Surely your priority is for a means to carry your own people along with your vision for their future, rather than what I might be able to seed into a foreign newspaper which most Austrian people could not read."

Keller this time: "We expect that there will be unrest in factories in the north leading up to the election. The government will shortly announce a new economic programme, which will affect prices and therefore the wages and living conditions of factory workers. The socialist party, who wish to stay part of the Alliance and keep their influence in the government will make empty promises to the manufacturing unions in return for their being no strikes. We believe that they will fail and there will be strikes on a large scale. There will also be the possibility that strikes become unrest which becomes violent through the actions of the nazis who are still a significant minority in our society."

Koplenig: "You see, it must not be interpreted that our party is stirring up unrest or encouraging others. We and our Soviet comrades wish to see a peaceful and orderly progression towards the Treaty and new beginning for Austria."

Keller: "We would like to arrange a visit for you to one or two factories in the north so that you can meet our comrades there and hear from them their honest endeavours to achieve a peaceful transition to the new independent Austria. We want you to be able to use your influence to convince the Western Allies that we are not a threat. We would like to be seen as a positive influence on the future of our country."

~~~

Events, hitherto unforeseen at FSS HQ, now happened in increasingly rapid succession.

Hugh was taken on a 2-day visit to the main industrial area of the Soviet zone and was the audience for what seemed to him to be a rehearsed listing of the Party's measures to limit subversive murmurings. He was present at a meeting where not all participants were introduced and the anonymous individuals mentioned two dates in September in the context of checking where and when and how their support would be required. This prompted the chairman to look quickly in his direction and satisfy himself that Hugh had not picked up the exchange. (In fact he had been engaged in a conversation with the person opposite him, but, using his now well-honed techniques, had convincingly shown no sign of noticing.)

The different branches of the Allies' Intelligence Services in Vienna had reacted with some alarm to the report which Hugh brought back. From security and policy aspects there were multiple implications and new unknowns. Certainly, it had been thought the Soviets were less inclined to see an excuse to march west and take over the whole of Austria and beyond (which they would have been well able to do militarily) as desirable in the short term, now that they had been occupied since the beginning of the year in a war in Korea. Nevertheless violent civil unrest would create a pretext if one were needed. Their case for this would be strengthened if nazis were seen to be actively connected. Violent civil unrest can only have two outcomes: either it must succeed, or its instigators must be seen to be discredited. Relations between the Soviet occupiers and the Austrian communist party were at best tepid, but Moscow would not want to see its doctrinal ally discredited. Equally, the Allies believed, it had no strong interest in a united and independent Austrian state via the Treaty, but was most likely intent on creating a puppet state out of eastern Austria along the lines it had recently achieved in Hungary and Czechoslovakia.

Between the British and the US central commands it was agreed that all available information should be passed to Herr Frigl, the President, first, while at commandant level soundings were to be made to determine the degree of cooperation there might be at this point between the Soviets and the KPÖ. Conversations were tentatively extended as far as determining that the Soviets would not wish strikes to ferment further disturbance and were primarily concerned with their negative effect on production targets, which would be liable to prompt interest from the Kremlin. But although the commandant Abakumov was represented at their meetings, there was no intention to overtly intervene. The British and US contacts were never able to determine how the Soviet attitude might change if they learnt that the KPÖ were almost certainly intending to involve 'clean' but disaffected nazis in the country, this being the information picked up by Hugh, together with the planned start date and locations in September.

Both the President and the Allies' central command were fearful that nazi involvement would not and could not be concealed and that it made more likely a dangerously unstable situation, particularly given the existence of freelance paramilitaries in the industrial areas (and even Vienna itself). But whereas the Allies would studiously avoid intervention, this would not be the case for the Russians, who, once mobilised would be likely to find reasons to extend their reach beyond the agreed zones.

At the beginning of September Herr Frigl personally authorised the police and certain paramilitary units to round up and detain all known nazi sympathisers in the north of the country. Strikes and demonstrations went ahead, but with the assistance of unions loyal to the socialist party, unrest was at a level that could be contained by the police and calls for a general strike went largely unheeded. The Russians made token gestures of support in a small number of factories and relations between them and the KPÖ sunk to a low level. Elections were held in October and confirmed popular support for Herr Frigl as President and for his coalition government.

~~~

Hugh knew that he was of no further use in his cover role of accredited Times reporter to the Intelligence Corps or to the Allies' central command. He asked to be returned to the 138th Infantry, from where he had been seconded, but was told that a transfer back was not "technically" possible at that juncture. He must stay put, minimise his time away from his rooms and change his routes. He must not frequent the same outside locations. Accordingly, he no longer went to any cafés, gave up the Musikverein and the Austrian Literary Society and only sat in open locations where he had good visibility all round.

When he was in his rooms he spent much of his time writing letters to Barbara, knowing very well that he would never send them because of the distress and anxiety they would cause her.

But this one he did send:

Letter from Hugh to Barbara 25th October 1949

Dear Barbara

Hope at last that all this will soon be over. I can't say very much, except that the assignment for which I was seconded has come to an end. I have done what I was required to do and the outcome has been positive and there is no more I have to do now except wait until I can come back, probably directly to England but I can't be certain of that. My official time is very nearly up so I assume that I won't be going back the way I came.

I mainly spend my time in my rooms, though they have told me they may find somewhere else for me for the last weeks before I leave. I read a lot (in English and German), I write (mainly travel reminiscences about my time in Austria), and I (try to) play the flute!

Yes, really, the other day I bought a second-hand flute in this very quaint old shop just off Operngasse. It was more of an antiquarian shop than a music shop, but he said it used to belong to the chief flautist in the Opera Orchestra... well, if you believe that.

Why the flute? They pack up small. It would be a bit tricky trying to bring a double bass back, wouldn't it? Anyway I like the gentle soothing sound of a flute. It shares the aura of a white cat I think.

So there you are, you can think of me playing haunting wistful melodies in my fourth floor garret in this beautiful damaged grandiose evocative spooky old lady which is Vienna... and looking forward, so looking forward, to seeing you once more.

Your loving,

Hugh

The following day Hugh's CO sent an NCO to Hugh's rooms at 5am with orders to bring him to FSS HQ. They were to leave enough lying around the rooms to look as if they were still being occupied and ensure that they leave Grashofgasse before first light, putting a light on behind them which would show under the door.

During the night the body of Herr Keller, who had vouched for Hugh and been responsible for his 2-day visit to Vöcklabruck and the neighbouring industrial facilities had been found in the Danube. He had been shot in the head. It was to Hugh's good fortune that the Russian commandant in the Central Command was prepared to be persuaded by the chairman of the communist party that this was the settling of a score, since Keller had been the sole link with full details of the recent disturbances. For Herr Koplenig it was preferable that the failure of the insurrection (which the Russians in any case did not want) had been betrayal from within, than that the Party had naïvely opened its doors to such a poorly disguised intruder as Hugh Winters.

FSS well knew that there was more than one interest group within the KPÖ as well as others outside it who had been disadvantaged by the thwarting of the link-up of the communists and the nazis and could have the means of tracing its source. It was decided that Hugh should go back in uniform, which, though it made him more conspicuous, could be a deterrent to any score settling. Arrangements would be made for him to be transferred to the UK, but in the meantime to be billeted in a safe house on the edge of the British zone until he was collected by a convoy for his return home.

Early in December he wrote what he believed would be his last letter to Barbara.

Letter from Hugh to Barbara 5th December 1949

Dear Barbara

Every day seems an age now. I have been told to stay in since I was moved out of Grashofgasse, though I have to go out occasionally of course. I am on my own in the new place too and so I do have to go out for food, but I am no longer frequenting cafés. I bought a few more books to replace those I had had to leave behind in Grashofgasse, mainly in German, but a couple in English, and I went into Kärntner Antiquitariat again and found another figurine which I hope you will like. If you thought the cat was symbolic of you, then this one must be me. It's a mountain goat, a buck, looking quite statuesque - there, I'm nothing if not vain! So I will get it sent when I go out for food today. I had seen it a few weeks ago, and I dithered but I kept on going back to it.

You know how it often seems like, the way life works, things can be so close to turning out completely different than the way they do. It would only need something to be minutely different... someone looking in a different direction, getting called just as you are about to cross the road, bumping into someone and stopping to help them... such small differences can change the world. And we never actually know. It was a bit like that with this mountain goat. I had been wondering for a few days whether I would buy it, not because I didn't want to send you a present, it was the symbolism thing, it did feel a bit vain, and that's definitely not you I know, so I had gone and sat in Stephansplatz to work it out and decide and I was contemplating the cathedral and letting myself get awed by its massive presence. Lost to the world I was. Then behind me from across towards the corner of the square came a low rumbling, it was difficult to tell whether it was a shaking or a noise. I looked round at the buildings along the square behind me - a lot of reinforcing has been going on, but that had stopped and in places there were walls 3 or 4 storeys high detached and standing on their own and I saw some bricks and stones come away from right at the top of one of these and fall. Then everything happened at once. People shouting, running, yelling, I saw that African girl standing looking up as the top part of the wall started to lean, then more stones and in slow motion, it seemed, it collapsed - screaming all around me now, the girl running towards me, and as the wall crumpled into a heap of rubble she stumbled into my arms.

Miraculously no-one was hurt, but the girl seemed more dishevelled and neglected than when I had last seen her. And she was in severe shock. She didn't say anything, but she let me take her to a refuge which I had got to know about. Being in uniform now, I thought that should be sufficient for me not to seem a risk, and it was ok, so that's where I left her. I knew she would be washed and clothed and fed and have somewhere to sleep and they said I could come by and check on her if I wanted. So I have done that regularly. The staff told me she hadn't said a word all the time she has been there, so they cannot even tell what language she speaks. She spends most of the day sitting in front of a window looking out.

She simply sits clutching her locket - which she won't allow anybody to look at - gazing out into the distance. They say that around the middle of the afternoon when she seems to sense that I might be coming, she goes to the big room by the entrance and sits with a book, facing the door. I go every day now. I talk to her, but she has never said a word. I have spent hours with her now and I don't even know her name. I tell her my name every time. She takes me to a window and we sit side by side looking out... in silence. I have never been a spiritual person, but it reminds me of how my father described that Quaker nurse he knew here in Vienna 30 years ago.

Alright, that's today's news story. More tomorrow or the next day. Maybe I can give you a tour of Vienna, a new part of the city each day. And then, when I am back, I can pull them all together into some kind of travel guide. Well, I'll have to find something to do, won't I? I can't be a kept man, I might drift into sloth and laziness. And I don't think that's the sort of man you would have much time for.

Loving good wishes,

Hugh

Barbara read the letter several times.

All that evening the picture of the collapsing wall and the girl running for her life kept coming back. Mixed in was another war-shattered wall falling, and somewhere another girl... Eva, yes, that was her name, Eva...

the last room

3rd. January 1941, 1.20am: Temple Back, Bristol

"Everywhere had gone quiet. It was eery. The drone of the bombers had faded into the distance. The clacking of our guns had stopped because they had nothing to fire at. The last lot of bombs had ripped apart roofs and crashed through floors and blasted out walls, shredded curtains, splintered glass... now there was just the hanging left... suspended artefacts of lost lives... still life of no life. Down the road there was another ambulance, camouflaged, but I could see the large red cross in the white circle, white, in the middle of this chaos?... a woman shouting, no, screaming "Eva"... someone in uniform looking up, pulling her, and another, trying to pull *her* away... then it came down with a sickening stomach-churning thud... the end-wall of the terrace. They were lifting me onto the stretcher now. I didn't see any more, but I have always wondered about them, those two women and Eva."

BRISTOL EVENING POST
EMERGENCY BULLETIN

Bristol lost historic buildings in a Nazi flare and flame raid which grew suddenly in intensity nearly an hour after the "alert" was sounded.

The "blitz" was heralded by flares dropped in different parts of the town although for some time there was little sign of a serious raid developing.

But the flares were the signal for a rain of incendiaries with a few petrol bombs and later high explosives. Fire fighting services were swiftly in action, augmented by ARP wardens, home guards...

Barbara's House: 5th December 2009

"No, there was no more white porcelain, just the cat and the buck. The buck was him, I think, and the white cat was me. All symbolic.

"It was 60 years ago exactly, the date on his last letter. That's how I came to remember her name, because he told me about seeing the end wall of a bombed building collapse unexpectedly and a girl running who just managed to escape and he had picked her up and taken her somewhere safe. It reminded me of the very beginning of 1941 and the Bristol Blitz. There was a girl then and her name came back to me suddenly, it was Eva, but I don't think she was so lucky as Hugh's girl.

"You know I was an ambulance driver? A secretary at the Ministry of Food during the day and ambulance driver at night. I was pretty hopeless at first, I couldn't keep them straight, great clumsy things, huge steering wheels and no power steering of course. Not made for girls. But I got the hang in the end and I was never completely stuck. Lucky, because sometimes they had to send us out drivers only - there could be crew lost on shift.

"It was so cold that night. Right at the beginning of January 1941. A Thursday. I think there was snow on the ground and it was iced over on the roads. We knew they were going to come for us soon. They were working down the country - Sheffield, Manchester, Birmingham - it would be Cardiff or us that night for certain, and it was us. I came on duty at 8 and in the middle of the raid. I was based at the Infirmary and the calls were all to Cotham, Hotwells, that side of the harbour and we were coping. Yes, we went out while the bombs were falling as well.

"Not long after midnight there was a lull. The explosions stopped, the drone of planes faded away, but the all-clear didn't sound. There was the din of human grief along the corridors, engines starting, people shouting orders, but behind all that, silence. It was quite unnerving. Waiting.

"That lasted an hour or so. And then they were back. It seemed even heavier, different planes. I heard my station chief giving someone a really hard time on the phone and when he finished he called us together, the few who hadn't already gone out, and told us the General Hospital had said they had stopped admitting because of overcrowding, so everything was coming to us. We had a couple of units waiting repair, but they still ran, so we were to man one-up per unit until further notice.

"Now my calls seemed to be all down through the city to the old wharf area, Redcliffe and Temple Back. In those days that area was a mixture of workshops, some tenement housing, small factories, a jumble of half-timbered buildings hundreds of years old and brick Victorian warehouses, all sorts, I didn't know it at all well. That was where I picked up this family, a mother and four boys aged between 5 and 12 I should think. Almost every building in the vicinity had been hit, piles of rubble were right across the road - I had had a job to get through. While I was picking them up a warehouse behind on the Floating Harbour was hit. The noise all round was like a train in a never-ending tunnel. Clouds and clouds of dust. Eyes streaming constantly, we couldn't see. We were staggering around with our arms across our faces. There wasn't anyone else in sight, the mother said ok, so finally I set off back. There were obstructions all along the route, but we got back eventually and I set them down in the holding area.

"We were allowed a cup of tea between calls. So I went down for mine. Some crew went straight back out, or tried to, but our chief wouldn't let us, he was pretty hot on keeping his people roadworthy as best he could. I had been there a few minutes on my own, trying not to look terrified, when there was this scream from back in the holding area. A woman's scream like I had never heard before. Then a babble of voices, everyone trying to calm her, but the screaming went on and on and no-one seemed to be able to help. It was the mother of the four boys I had just brought in. It had to be. I went back and there was general pandemonium, but the mother recognised me and came over and clung on to me crying desperately, "Take me back, please take me back, we didn't have my daughter." I looked across to the Chief. He glared back at me, "Don't even ask. It's getting heavier down there. NO-ONE is leaving here until it eases. Not for anything." But the mother went on screaming and crying, most of the children in the hallway were crying, one or two adults started to show their displeasure at this person who couldn't hold herself together... I tried the Chief again. I said I knew where to go and I could be there and back quicker than anyone. Eventually he relented on the strict condition that I went to where I picked them up, put her down and returned immediately. It was up to the police then.

"I wasn't being quite honest when I said I knew where to go. I thought I should, but another few buildings hit and everything looked different. And you had nothing to see by except the fires. You were driving between flickering shadows on a cloudy night like that night. But we made it and I got down from the ambulance with her and followed her towards where she thought her daughter had gone, "probably looking for her cat", she had said on the way and now she started shouting "Eva" over and over again. She was scrambling over piles of rubble but I could see this gable wall standing on its own and it was swaying at the top so I went after her and was trying to pull her away, but then I was being pulled as well. The mother slipped from my grasp and I was being dragged back into my van and someone else was in the driving seat and he was turning us round. He was in ARP uniform and he shouldn't be driving my ambulance. I asked him who he was, I would report him, and he said, "My name is Norman and you can't be here, it has got too dangerous." I turned to look out of the back window. My stomach churned as the wall collapsed. It was like slow motion and I felt sick. I couldn't see the mother now, but I thought I saw something white moving in the clouds of dust thrown up by the collapse. Then again faintly, "Eva, Eva." Then nothing.

"I never found out what happened, but even today I can still hear that mother's cry, over and over. It haunts me. I think Eva means life. I hope it did that night.

"I never told them at home. Somehow it felt personal. I would have told *him*, Hugh, I nearly did in the last letter I sent him, but it seemed a bit, well, indelicate somehow, after all he had been through. I would have told him in the end, though.

"If he had come. But he didn't.

"So I've told you.

"Oh… his name wasn't really Hugh, by the way."

leaving now

5th December 2021

It was the last night I spent in the house. I had been all round now and I was ready to leave.

Barbara left her married home and moved into her caravan in January 1950. There she waited, but no word ever came. A few years later when I visited, she had acquired a white cat - "It just wandered in," she said, "and stayed." A stray? "Perhaps". She called it Lîla, short for Turangalîla she told me. In 1969 she re-married, to a work colleague, a Lancastrian, who was a perfect fit for the passionate bee-keeper she had become. Gone, finally, the turmoil and the uncertainty, the yearning and the regret. Gone now the wondering.

This play is finished. The house - the stage - can resume its plain drapes; no more scene changes needed, those props can be put away, the action is over.

But leave the white cat. It will find its own way.

~~~

I hadn't heard the post come and I was on my way out for the last time when I found the letter on the doormat. It was one of those old-style flimsy airmail envelopes, the sort that you wrote on the inside and then folded along the dotted lines to allow you to stick it down and put the address in the right place. It was very tattered and there were several hands in evidence amongst an assortment of markings. Sundry official stamps, the most prominent saying:

BFPO RELEASE: DATE REDACTED

The original postage stamp had been torn off along with most of the original franking. I looked for the place of posting but this was too smudged to read and as for the date I could only make out the figure 50. You hear of letters turning up decades after they were posted, but for this one to have been delivered here this morning was certainly serendipitous. The address was this address, though that was written on a fairly recent label stuck on top of what had been there before, but the addressee, just a first name, was clear and in a hand which was familiar -

Barbara

I opened it, and a shiver ran down my spine...

Vienna   *5th January 1950*

Dearest Barbara

It is over now, just the waiting left until the convoy arrives in the morning. I will be able to post this at the barracks and it will get to England before I do.

Our arrival date is uncertain because we are likely to have a great many holdups along the way.

After all the clamour of the last days it is uncannily quiet here. I used to be uneasy when I suddenly noticed silence, as you know, but tonight I think I'm ok with it. Time to myself, just musing.

Things come up you don't expect. The name of the Quaker nurse my father had worked with in Vienna came back to me. Do you remember? You asked me what her name was, though you were a bit vague about it, your Aunt Louie was something to do with it, I think. Anyway, it was Isabella.

I cannot deny that to finally leave my Vienna life will be a wrench. No, not the life exactly, for the life is terrifying if you let yourself feel it, no, the people, my people, now I'm back with them. To be back in uniform was a bit like a coming home.

And would you believe?... that young girl I found all those weeks ago wandering around Stephans Platz on her own all dazed and dishevelled and then again after she was almost crushed by a wall - I was so pleased I could get her into that refuge, I don't know what would have happened to her otherwise - but yesterday, after all those weeks of silence, she spoke! She told me her name - Nobomi. She said she was looking for her cat, it was a white cat called Umzuli. She even let me see the locket she always grasps so tightly and said it was her grandmother's, who was also called Nobomi. She had a photograph of her grandmother as well - as an attractive young African woman in a striking white and black dress. I was puzzled by the names, but we have a native South African in our unit and he said they are Xhosa names - Nobomi means life and Umzuli means wanderer. A Xhosa girl in Vienna? And that locket was strange. It looked very old and the picture inside was a faded sepia photograph, but it was a picture of a very English-looking lady, holding a white cat! I tried to find a way to bring her back with me, but it was just not going to be possible. Trouble is, it feels like I am leaving a part of _me_ behind. We had shared all those hours of silence and I was so much wanting to be able to look out for her.

They say these things pass. I wonder.

You know I have one drop to make when I get back to Blighty, then, it's just us. Shall we have tea in the Pump Rooms?

Your ever loving,
Hugh

the end

Family Tree

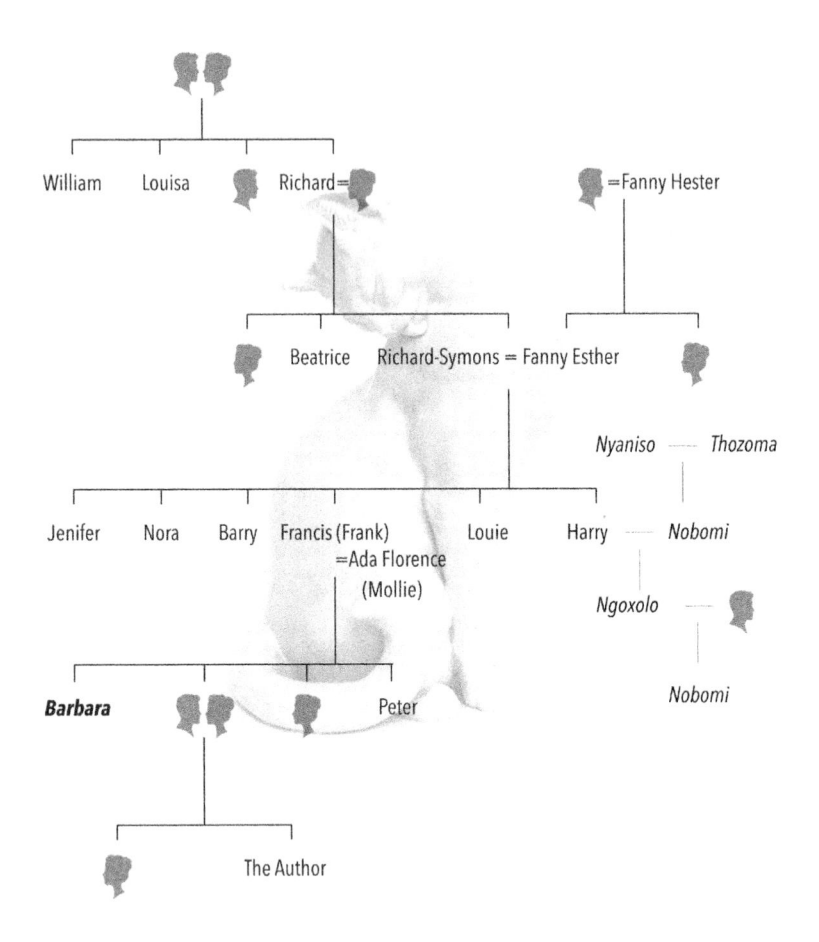

William Louisa Richard = ⬥ ⬥ = Fanny Hester

Beatrice Richard-Symons = Fanny Esther

Nyaniso —— *Thozoma*

Jenifer Nora Barry Francis (Frank) = Ada Florence (Mollie) Louie Harry —— *Nobomi*

Ngoxolo ——

Barbara Peter

Nobomi

The Author

Acknowledgements

For an author to acknowledge all those who have contributed, for the most part unwittingly, to any of her or his works, would be an impossibility. Such is the complexity of human interaction and influences that to light on one or another would have to be down to happenstance.

Nevertheless I must mention with gratitude the considerable help on all matters connected with the Society of Friends and Isabella Davy that I have received from Ackworth School in Yorkshire (which Isabella attended from 1881 to 1886) and particularly their archivist Celia Wolfe, who was also good enough to read an early version of the chapters containing their ex-pupil. For the Xhosa translations and other help, I am indebted to Vumile Kempeni, as well as the services of Polilingua.

I am grateful to Martin George for locating the municipal record of the death of Harry in East London. Information on that town, Cape Colony and South Africa at the turn of the nineteenth century has been aided by Tabitha Jackson and Will Bennett. There was also a limited amount of family archive relating to East London and Cape Colony.

Information about postwar Vienna has been drawn from a number of published and anecdotal sources, in particular the work of Warren Wellde Williams of the University of Wales in Swansea and of Panagiotis Dimitrakis from King's College London. In addition I have made extensive use of the National Archives at Kew.

~~~

If you have enjoyed reading White Cat
look out for its sequel –
AND THEN THERE ARE THE STORIES
expected early 2023.

About the author

Simon Cole lives with his wife in the foothills of the Pyrenees Mountains in south-west France. He has been a psychological therapist and trainer for over 35 years. In 2007 he moved from the UK to create a retreat centre in a location which would offer a setting for 'therapeutic release', using the area's natural grandeur as a backdrop for meditation, music, walking and mindfulness.

After many articles in professional journals and online, and books on therapy, meditation and philosophy, "White Cat" was his first venture into a genre of reflective fiction anchored in real lives and events. "Then There Are The Stories" is its sequel and draws on the mystical layer which lies behind our everyday lives.

book website: www.stillnessinmind.com
email: simon.cole.france@icloud.com

Printed in Great Britain
by Amazon